The Organist Who Wore Gloves

another Green Mountain whodunit
in the Alex and Ms. Mulholland series

Elaine Magalis

This is a work of fiction. All characters and events portrayed in this book are fictitious and not intended to represent real people or places.

Although the locale where this story takes place is a real one, various liberties have been taken, and this book does not purport to offer an exact depiction of any particular place or location.

Copyright © 2012 Elaine Magalis

All rights reserved.

ISBN-13: 978-1480258532

To the ghosts we wished we'd met,
but never did.

Acknowledgments

Thanks to those who have read this book in manuscript, and made suggestions and corrections, especially Paula Behnken, Maureen James, Virginia Jenkins and Cathie Lyons. Special thanks, as always, to Jeannine Young who proofread it!

Preface

After I wrote *The Body in the Butter Churn*, I heard again and again that the book should be one in a series, especially if it truly was a "cozy mystery." As it turned out, it wasn't hard to write a second book. I found that I had further ambitions for Alex and Ms. Tasha Mulholland. I wanted them both to get older; I wanted them to be funkier and more troubled. I wanted them to reflect on their friendship as a twelve-going-on-thirteen-year-old boy and an elderly woman-but-not-a-grandmother. I also hoped that their next case would be more fantastic, like the museum where it all began.

I think I've managed some of that.

Elaine Magalis

The Organist Who Wore Gloves

The Organist Who Wore Gloves

I

The student bedroom was bright with spring light filtering through the still unleafed elm trees. Alex Churchill listened to the whistling of chickadees, and shivered. The Old Shrubsbury School Museum was cold. Winter still hung around the windows. It had been there for months, so everything was silent and unmoving, as if the museum building were ice-bound, frozen in time and place with no past or future, only a very long present. He wondered, as he had before, how students at the school had lived through the nineteenth century winters with nothing in their rooms to warm themselves except tiny fireplaces for charcoal from the kitchen chimney downstairs.

Alex had been enlisted to begin cleaning on the second floor in preparation for a May Day museum opening. He was saving money for a new bike or he wouldn't have been here, not even for Tasha Mulholland, not even in the student room, where he'd always enjoyed doing time travel. There were windows on two sides, and like a student from long ago, he could look down the tree-lined road to see who was coming. An uncle who lived in the village? Schoolmaster Reverend Timothy Evensong returning from a visit to a neighbor? Ms. Mulholland walking her dog, Gusty? He and Ms. M had placed books by a hypothetical student's bedside, and put real charcoal in his fireplace. His pretend clothes hung from a hook. A daguerreotype of someone who could have been his mother was on his bedside table.

But it was too cold.

Worse, something was wrong with the room—either that or Alex was catching a mental hypothermia from the cold. The rope bed looked slept in. The fireplace had embers that were more than make-believe—they were turning to ashes. The student's books had been rearranged.

He started to go downstairs to talk to Ms. M about

it, but stopped to look in at Timothy Evensong's study, the second room at the front of the building, just in case there was more to report. The Reverend Evensong had built the four-story granite school dormitory almost two centuries before with the help of a single ox. It was said that the beast either wouldn't or couldn't come down from the four story building when the job was done, so he was roasted in place for a celebratory dinner. Evensong's study held things that had been his all those years ago: an oxbow, a static electricity machine, books, slates and chalk, his desk with its inkwell and a perfect goose feather of a pen standing upright in it. The daguerreotypes of the good Reverend and his wife were on one wall and student artwork on another. Above the desk, a stuffed owl watched everything silently, waiting for its chance to pounce. Ms. M had warned that the bird was moldering and would soon be consigned to the rubbish heap, but it seemed to have made it through the winter one more time.

Alex was about to go back to the student room and give his fevered brain another chance, when he noticed that the slate globe, that most wonderful blackboard, had been marked up in chalk. Someone had been in Timothy Evensong's study!

"Yes, I know, "said Tasha Mulholland when he told her. "The fireplace in the kitchen has been used. Someone drank from a glass and ate from a plate. I don't know who. No one has a key except for the director and me, and Lori wouldn't want to camp out here in the winter. No one would."

"They'd have to be crazy."

"I know." She sighed deeply. "It's a mystery, Alex. Maybe our famous detective duo could solve it. Do you want to try?"

"Yep. Absolutely. It makes me mad. The museum doesn't belong to some homeless guy looking for shelter. Do you think?"

"He'd be better off almost anywhere else."

Tasha was dusting the ancient china that filled a nineteenth century sideboard. Alex reluctantly joined her. Dusting was no job for a guy, but he was lucky to be here at all. His mother had only just relented. She'd been looking for a job for him in the general store, since she figured it was relatively safe. No murder had ever taken place there. Of course, the murder of Old Aggie last autumn had been a first in the long history of the Old Shrubsbury School Museum, and Alex would learn much more working with Ms. M than with the grocer who knew nothing about anything but foodstuffs and lottery tickets. Point made, and decisively, she'd given in, but with a caveat: the moment he and Ms. M began to investigate anything even vaguely criminal, he was out, even if it meant he had to stay at home all summer.

Unfazed, the two sleuths decided to go from room to room, searching for more evidence. First, they went through the kitchen. Someone had put water in the chimney basin. It was still damp. They went through the closet. Someone had borrowed a flashlight—unless Alex or Ms. M had misplaced it.

It was in the music room that they found the strangest piece of evidence. The organ bench had been left at an odd angle, as if someone had been playing the instrument and forgotten to push it back to where it usually stood, perfectly parallel to the organ. Was someone playing their Estey organ? Of course, it might be tempting to try. With its incised fruits and vines and its many-colored pipes, with some carved god of music or other at the top where it peaked, it was beautiful; surely it would sound just as lovely as it looked. Still, the only one who ever tried to play it was Cornelia Early, the board's treasurer, and there was no reason why she would have done it on a winter night.

"The bench probably just got bumped last fall," said Alex.

"Maybe," said Ms. M, but she was distracted, as if she heard something, maybe music, as if there were someone playing the old organ at that very minute.

"What is it, Ms. M?"

"I remember waking up last week in the middle of the night and hearing the Bach 'Toccata and Fugue in D Minor.' I thought it was just my audio imagination. The 'Toccata' is kind of a musical cliché, but I was pleased to think I'd been listening to music in my sleep. Thinking back, it sounded like the Estey, as if it took more energy to play than newer, bigger organs. The piece is way too big for a little parlor organ like this so I was certain it was a dream, and besides, who would be in the museum at two or three a.m., when the temperature is polar, playing the organ—especially this one?"

"Something weird is going on!"

"Well, it couldn't have been Cornelia. She doesn't play well enough to even attempt that piece. I'll try to listen at night from now on."

The Organist Who Wore Gloves

"Won't you be scared to be alone if the phantom organ player comes again?"

"Oh, no. If the phantom plays Bach, he must be a friend."

Oh, sure, thought Alex. And probably a little dull besides. Why couldn't the intruder be one of the guys from Aerosmith? I'll bet not all the players of Bach are friends.

"I'll stay with you. What if he's dangerous?"

"I don't think your mother will agree to that, Alex. You're only just allowed to be here weekend days since we went after Old Aggie's murderer. She's not going to go for an overnighter."

"I could sneak out. She'd never know."

"I'd know," Ms. M said grimly.

Alex sighed. A grown up wouldn't have to put up with this kind of stuff. "Promise me you won't let the phantom know you're watching, no matter what. You'll only just peek and wait to tell somebody. And I'll be the first somebody!"

"Agreed," said Ms. Mulholland. "I have no desire to

meet anyone strange enough to play a pump organ at below freezing."

They continued working until Alex remembered: "The phantom wrote something on the chalkboard globe. Maybe it's a clue."

Together, they went to Evensong's study and put on the white gloves Ms. M always carried with her to protect the old things on exhibit. Sitting on the wide windowsill, they studied the slate ball.

The squatter had used the crudely cut pieces of chalk that lay nearby. Even though everyone talked about students trying to map the world in chalk, no one living ever had. Until now, Alex had never seen any marks on the ball. These marks were words. "Spirit. Lightning. Time...."

"He's written a poem," said Ms. M. "I can't make it out without my glasses. What do you see, Alex?"

Alex read with his voice full of hesitation, not sure what the man was talking about but suspicious of some of the words:

O the joy of my spirit! it is uncaged! it darts like lightning!

The Organist Who Wore Gloves

It is not enough to have this globe, or a certain time—

I will have thousands of globes, and all time.

"Why, it's from Walt Whitman's 'Poem of Joy.' I used to love that poem. Our phantom is a person of culture. And a happy one at that."

"Humph," muttered Alex. "The globe's not for putting poems on. You know it. I know it. Why doesn't he?"

"Or she."

"Yeah. Or she. Why would the phantom write a poem on the globe?"

"I have an assignment for you, Alex."

"Yeah I saw it coming. I'll read the whole poem this weekend. I promise. I'd like to try to figure this guy out."

They went from room to room but nothing else had been disturbed. There was no sign that the intruder had slept on any of the rope beds or under the crazy quilt. If he or she had spent time in the library, the books were still in the same order. The paintings on the wall were in their same places. The loom hadn't been touched and none of the tall clocks had been wound up. He wasn't in the woven casket on the second floor.

When they left, they locked the front door carefully before they went to look for Lori Chickering, the interim director of the Old Shrubsbury School Museum.

Lori hadn't a clue about the organ-playing phantom, and insisted on making bad jokes about him. "Oh, Tasha. Books disarranged, an organ bench askew. You're making up things. You and Alex are bored. You want another murder. It's not going to happen. Not in Shrubsbury." She laughed her neighing laugh, and Cornelia Early, the museum's treasurer who was sharing tea and peanut butter sandwiches with her, chuckled in a deep rumble that always made Alex's toes curl. In combination, their laughs were especially painful.

"Someone wrote some verse by Walt Whitman on the slate globe in Evensong's room," Tasha muttered. She didn't like being laughed at.

"Some mischievous tourist from last fall," said Cornelia brightly, her blue eyes guffawing at them both. "You know the museum in the winter and early spring is entirely too uncomfortable for a squatter or a music lover. For anyone at all."

The Organist Who Wore Gloves

"Ah, well. You needn't believe us. But something odd is going on."

"A ghost!" laughed Lori.

Sure, thought Alex. Why not? Grown ups who worked in history museums should believe in ghosts. If they'd worked in them long enough, they should have seen one. Maybe more. And if they hadn't, well, as far as he was concerned, they were deaf, blind and might as well be dumb, like those "Hear no evil, see no evil, speak no evil" Japanese monkeys.

II

For a few nights after, in her apartment on the second floor of the Cyril Benning House across the lawn from the museum, Tasha waited for the organist. Huddled in a crazy quilt, she listened by an only slightly opened window, drank her new favorite coffee–Dark Wisdom–and read poems by Walt Whitman. From time to time, she thought she saw a light flicker in the windows, like a candlestick being walked from room to room, but decided that she was imagining it. Give Lori and Cornelia their due. There were probably no such beings as ghosts, and certainly no humans in the museum on a night when the temperature had slipped to below freezing by ten o'clock.

But one night someone started playing the "Toccata and Fugue" again, the old Estey wheezing and stuttering as the notes climbed up and down the hallways of the museum. How did the player keep so many in the air at once with such a pitiful instrument or was she just hearing them because she knew the music? Tasha pulled on jeans under her nightgown, wrapped herself in an old parka, grabbed a flashlight and headed down the stairs and out into the night. A small band of moon glittered on the horizon. Wind whispered in the trees, playing snare drums with the music, making it almost as grand as she'd ever heard it. The night was a concert hall.

To her amazement, the big wooden door to the museum was open, and she slipped into the building. By then—even before then—the music was changing in some way she couldn't understand. It was being overcome by something like a jitterbug. That Estey, she thought. It can't even get through a few measures of Bach without revising everything. The floors were trembling as if someone in big boots was stomping up and down the hallways. Even though she couldn't have been heard by anyone, man or spirit, she crept down the hall to the door of the music room. As she raised her light, she saw him for just an instant—a thin, pale man in an overcoat with copper buttons, blinking in the sudden glow, his gloved hands raised over the keys.

As suddenly as the music had begun, it stopped. She heard him stumbling away from the instrument and running into the kitchen and out the kitchen door. All that remained was the sound of his footsteps, light and quick, and the glistening windows. A bicycle rolled down the road. By the time she reached the front door and looked out, he was gone.

Tasha went back to the organ and slid onto the bench. There was no printed music. He apparently knew the Bach by heart. But what an odd instrument to try and play, where it was all you could do to make simple hymns sound. She'd tried playing a rag on the organ years ago. The notes sank to the floor and dissolved there, one by one.

She went to the kitchen and looked around with her flashlight, hoping that he'd left something that would give him away. His presence was still so real. If she hadn't heard him leave, she'd think he was here, perhaps in the rocking chair in Evensong's study, waiting for her to go, or maybe in the student room, sitting on a sill, looking out at the setting moon. She liked this man, whoever he was.

Alex, however, was exasperated. His partner had

caught sight of the museum phantom. Why hadn't she waited in the shadows until he was finished? Ms. M was usually clever, but she'd clearly been led astray by the music. She hadn't been able to think. She'd let him get away. Not only had she failed miserably, she couldn't figure out a way for her partner to spend the night and listen with her. His problems with adults were insurmountable—his vocabulary word for the day from Ms. M.

"What can I do?" he complained to his friend Coker at lunchtime. They were lounging on a bench in the playing field, hanging out. "She's not going to find out who he is, not at this rate. I'm afraid she's happy to let him keep playing music and scribbling poetry on the globe. Since it's Bach, you know, she thinks he's a good guy and can come and go as he pleases."

"Ah, come on, Alex. You want him arrested for acting arty in the museum?"

"We don't know that that's all it is. Something really eerie could be going on."

"Yeah, I suppose. The guy is nuts, that's for sure." Coker stood up and stopped a ball as it did a slow bounce across the grass. "You wanna camp out there

Friday night?" he raised his voice. "The weather's warmed up a lot." He kicked the ball back and over the head of the anxious fourth-grader who'd come to retrieve it.

"Yeah, I guess it's not too bad if you have a sleeping bag. But didn't we make an oath we'd never do that?"

"Yeah, but we're older now. We know there's no such thing as ghosts. Don't we?"

"Yeah, maybe." Alex looked moodily across the playing field to the forest beyond. "I'm not really sure," he said.

"So you think this guy could be a ghost? Even so, he'd be a harmless enough spook, wouldn't he? Just playing the organ and writing poetry. Let's do it. Let's have a sleepover in the museum. I'll say I'm staying with you; you'll tell your mom you're staying with me. We'll roll out a couple of sleeping bags in the music room, and wait. Whadaya think?"

Alex pondered the problem and murmured a quick "eenie meenie miney mo."

This spring the museum was more important to him than ever. It was home. The ugly trailer he shared with his mother seemed more uncomfortable every year. His room was only a cubbyhole. Worse, he was embarrassed by the place. Most of his friends had houses with washers and dryers, at least two television sets, and an extra bedroom.

While history continued to be a fraught subject and the future seemed to him to be much more exciting than the past, he'd learned that imagination was as important to the one as to the other. The museum was a place full of stories, and he loved stories more than ever. How many kids could claim a home like this: big, full of lives, and stuff—really weird stuff?

He stood up and gazed across the playing field to the school building. School was almost out for the summer. It would be like a new beginning. He'd always been afraid of the museum at night. It was time he showed some guts.

"Let's do it," he said, and he and Coker high-fived.

"I don't know if you want to tell Ms. Mulholland or not," Coker said.

"Not. She likes this guy too much already. And I can't trust her not to tell things to my mom."

III

That Friday Alex borrowed one of Ms. M's keys when she wasn't looking. The day was just turning to dusk when the boys stole into the museum and set up camp in the kitchen. The phantom might come in through the kitchen door; he might come through the front. Whatever, they were ready for him.

They played Doom on their laptops for the first hour, but because they didn't want to waste battery power, and because the temperature was dropping fast, they stopped to break out sandwiches and popcorn then curled up in their sleeping bags. They told each other stories about scary things, things that had happened to them and things they'd heard about: The neighbor who was a werewolf by night and played with Coker's dog when the moon was full, the graveyard that emptied out every evening so that some corpses grew confused and returned to lie under the wrong stones, Old Aggie coming back to turn her daughter Sera's butter sour so that she couldn't eat it. By 9, at what was their weekday bedtime, they began to talk about the ghostly organ player. That's when everything got strange.

"Tell me about him, Alex. Who do you think this guy is?"

"Well, he's kind of like the guy in 'The Phantom of the Opera,' you know? Only there's no beautiful singer he's hot on, and the place is ice cold. He's gotta be crazy, or he wouldn't hang around a place that gets as cold as this one."

"Yeah. He's not here every night, is he?"

"Not as far as we know. My luck, he won't show tonight."

"Maybe he has a reason for coming some nights and not others."

"Yeah. Maybe some nights are like an anniversary or something."

"You mean, he comes because something happened on the same day some other time."

"Yeah."

"Like what do you think?"

"Well, it might be something musical. Maybe he used to play the Estey when the museum was a boarding house."

"It's not much of an organ. It's ancient. And the boarding house would have been an awful long time ago. Right?"

"Yeah, but what if he was playing at the same time his wife died, or a kid, or maybe his mother or father?"

"And he's trying to charm their spirits and make them come back."

"Could be."

"Maybe he murdered someone and then played the Estey."

"Maybe he did it in the museum."

"Nah. Not another murder in the museum. That could never happen."

"Why not? Old Aggie was killed just on the other side of that door." They both looked over at the door to the root cellar. They'd been ignoring it. "He could be related to her."

"Maybe we should wait in the next room instead."

"Yeah. Just in case." They gathered up everything and dragging their sleeping bags behind them, took up their watch again by the horsehair sofa in the middle of the long exhibit room next door.

"How did Ms. M describe this guy?"

"He was pale as a ghost with huge dark eyes. He wore an overcoat and he rode a bicycle."

"People don't wear overcoats here. They wear them in big cities. Here they wear parkas."

"Yeah. That's what I thought. And they don't wear overcoats when they bicycle. Ms. M guessed he was thin because his footsteps were light when he ran."

"He wouldn't have had to run if he was a dangerous dude with a gun or something."

"Maybe not."

"So we've got nothing to worry about. He's just a skinny guy who can't find an organ anywhere else."

"Most churches have one."

"Yeah, but he wouldn't want to be in a church. I mean, what if God caught him or the priest or someone? And if he's a spirit, it's even worse. I mean the place is holy. It's probably crawling with angels. He wouldn't want to be caught there."

"I don't think he'd come here if there wasn't something besides the organ. I mean there aren't any angels, but it's crazy. It's cold."

"Do you think he plays the organ with gloves on?"

"Oh yeah."

"The music must be awful."

"Well, I couldn't say, but Ms. M says it's not. He's probably been to college. Don't forget he puts Walt Whitman poems on the globe."

"An English major and a smart guy. Remember, a lot of geniuses are crazy."

"Maybe he comes to meet someone dead—you know, the ghost of Rev. Evensong or something."

"You do think there are ghosts living here, don't you?"

"Yeah. Just be quiet a minute and watch and listen. Then tell me you don't think so."

The boys hunkered down in their sleeping bags, listening. Something skittered down the stairs. A mouse? A chipmunk? A smallish raccoon? A smallish ghost? The moon was shining and tree branches were dancing at the windows, groping at the glass, trying to get in. Some kind of animal—maybe one of the great owls—screeched and screamed. Or maybe it was one of those catamounts the experts said had gone extinct in Vermont a century ago. Maybe a lost soul, tossed out of heaven, or escaped over the gateway from hell. Had they left the door open for the phantom guy? Should they have?

A spider spun down from the ceiling to a place between them, dangling on its silk rope, bouncing as if it were laughing at them. They heard footsteps in the kitchen, someone fooling with pots and pans, a murmur of voices, someone else picking out a hymn tune on the Estey. The Estey? Was anyone there, playing it? It was as if there were generations of dead people, living in the museum.

Someone was at the big oak door, turning a key,

pushing his way in, hesitating, walking down the hallway towards them.

Alex ducked further into his bag, Coker muttered "Jeeze!" They both stopped breathing.

"Hi Alex. Coker. Relax. It's only ten o'clock. You have a long night ahead of you." Ms. M stood at the door, shadowy in her flashlight glow. "I brought oatmeal cookies."

"Bejesus, Ms. Mulholland. You scared us to death. How did you know we were here?" asked Coker.

"I have my ways."

"I should have known you'd figure it out," muttered Alex. "You're not going to tell my mother, are you?"

"I'll keep quiet, Alex. You should have told her yourself. If you pull too many of these things, you'll be put under house arrest."

She walked over to the two boys in their bags, and put a dish of cookies on the floor between them. "I'm going to leave these. I brought a walkie talkie on the plate with them. I want you to alert me if anything happens. Got it?"

"Yeah. There's no signal up here," Alex explained to Coker. "We can't use cell phones most of the time. It's all random."

"It's like stepping back in time," murmured Coker.

"Yeah," said Alex. "Thanks Ms. M."

No sooner had she got there than she was gone again and they were on their own.

They dozed. It might have been about midnight when Alex woke up to find Coker pulling on his Nikes. "Gotta take a leak," he said, and headed to the front door. Alex waited until he came back. "Me too," he said. "Did you use the necessary?"

"You kidding?" said Coker. "I wouldn't go into an outhouse at this hour. All the spiders are working there."

Alex took his turn outside. Only he used the outhouse. As awful as it was at night, it was what people used to use and he figured he owed them the same respect. He paused at the front door before going back in. The strange animal had stopped screaming. The only owl was very far away now, probably somewhere down the road near his house. But by the pond across the road, he heard voices, inarticulate, soft. A man, a woman, another man. Why would anyone be there at this hour?

He began to creep, then walk, then creep again across the road, and down past the barn, sliding on the wet cold grass, until he was looking out over the pond. The figures were dim, even though part of a moon was high in the sky. They were standing directly below him on the dock arguing. He could see their gestures, their leaning toward each other, then away, like they were dancing hip hop. He tried to hear, but he could only catch a few words and phrases: "money... my business... everyone... no, never... I don't want to go to prison." One of the men was arguing with the woman. The other man, a man in an overcoat, watched them, his head bobbing from side to side, as one spoke and then the other. Finally, he shrugged his shoulders and, without saying a word, turned and began walking up the hill toward Alex and the museum. Alex darted back across the road, down the hallway, and into his sleeping bag.

"The guy is coming," he said in a loud whisper. "He's on his way."

The Organist Who Wore Gloves

"You're kidding," replied Coker.

"He's almost here." They both listened as the phantom organist walked into the building. But instead of going into the music room, he went up the stairs, and into the Rev. Evensong's room.

"He's going to write on the damn globe again," whispered Alex. "He's going to erase his Whitman and put up some other literary giant. Crap!"

"Whatareyougonnado?" asked Coker, pop-eyed.

"I dunno. The people outside were talking about going to jail. Maybe we'd better keep quiet and wait."

"You could call Ms. Mulholland. She'd know what to do."

She would. He knew Coker was right. So he buried himself in his sleeping bag and called her from inside. "He's here." That's all he said. Then he worried: What if the people outside were dangerous? What if they saw her coming and tried to hurt her? What if the phantom organist did?

The man upstairs would be able to see her from the window. Alex knew he was already looking, he was sure of it. He imagined him catching sight of her. Had he dropped the globe? Was that it rolling across the floor? The phantom came down the stairs double time, tumbling at the bottom, lurching out the door. Running. Alex and Coker squirmed out of their sleeping bags and ran down the hall to watch the shadowy form disappear into the bushes. Somewhere, a bicycle rattled into the night. The guy didn't even have a decent bike.

Ms. M strode into view, her lantern lit now, and swinging from her hand. "He got away, didn't he?"

"There's someone else across the road. He was with them," Alex said, and started for the barn and the pond with Ms. M and Coker at his heels.

But when he got to the barn, when he looked down at the pond, there was no one there. "They were there. Just at the edge of the pond," he said. "The other two were arguing while the organist listened. They talked about money, and the woman said she didn't want to go to prison."

Ms. M started down the bank. When she reached the pond, she looked around, into the bushes and even into the water. The boys joined her, and after all three had stared out into the night for a few minutes, they went to the dock and sat down. "They're gone now," she said. "Where, we don't know. I didn't hear any cars, did you? Just the bike. Did you recognize anyone, Alex?"

"It was too dark. And they were soft talkers, even though they were arguing. The woman seemed familiar, but I can't say why."

"I don't know how they got away without making some kind of disturbance, unless they went into the barn. Or headed for the parking lot."

"Let's look in the barn!" said Coker, and the boys made a dash for it. They had to wait for Ms. M—who couldn't or maybe just didn't want to run—and then they couldn't find anyone, not in the stalls or the loft. Not in the mangers. The barn was quiet and sweet smelling; no one had been in it. They sat down together on the edge of a harvester, cold and discouraged. They heard a car leaving from the parking lot on the other side of Evensong's house.

Sadly, the trio trudged over to Ms. M's apartment. She made cocoa, and they warmed themselves by her space heater and tried to think.

"It seems to me," she said, "that we should look at

the dock and the parking lot in the morning, before anything else goes on there. There seemed to have been only one car. Did one of the men and the woman leave together?"

"And at Evensong's room in the museum," said Alex, "that organist guy was there writing something on the slate globe. He may have broken it. I think I heard it roll."

"If he broke it, I'll change my mind about him," said Ms. M.

IV

Very early in the morning, before the boys headed home, they went with Ms. M to study the parking lot and the pond, but there were no prints they could distinguish from any others, and no one had dropped a clue. The slate globe hadn't rolled across the floor, but the organist had erased his poem and inscribed a new message. "The cheater and her assistant. Try asking them about their lives. See if you get…." Presumably, at this point, Tasha Mulholland's approach had scared him and he'd run.

"What does he mean, Ms. M? It doesn't have anything to do with the last quotation, does it?"

"It doesn't seem to."

"I think he's warning us about the people across

the road. The woman who didn't want to go to prison and the other guy."

"Perhaps so. Work on your memory and see if you can come up with something. You said the woman seemed familiar."

"Yeah, but I can't get closer than that."

"None of your teachers?"

"Not again. Thank God, no."

"Anyone who works at the museum—like Lori, for example?"

"No, I'd recognize Lori's voice anywhere."

"Yes. It is different," she said. "Although, if she's not laughing, it's almost any voice. Just think about the voices and the images today, Alex. See if you remember anything else."

Alex didn't come up with anything in the days that followed. Neither did Tasha. The phantom organist didn't reappear, and everything was quiet in the Old Shrubsbury School Museum. They finally cleaned off the slate globe, although Tasha kept notes about the Whitman poem and the last odd words the phantom

The Organist Who Wore Gloves

had written. The weather gradually warmed, the trees were filling out and billowing in the spring breezes. The museum building straightened its great granite shoulders and looked proud. Inside everything was in good form, waiting for the first visitors. The Star butter churn that had played such a terrible role in the previous season's murder had been cleaned and brought back by Sheriff Mulholland, although Lori agreed that if too many visitors asked about its role in the murder of Old Aggie, they'd put it in storage.

It was the last day of school and Alex despaired of it more than ever. There was so much to learn and so little the teachers seemed to teach. He was grateful that it was finally over, that he would no longer have to sit still for hours, learning things he already knew. He and his mother had discussed the situation many times, but they couldn't afford to send him somewhere because all the somewheres seemed to be expensive. Only rich young men and women were to be spared all that boredom.

For some of the year, he'd been eager to become a soccer hero, but even that possibility had gone flat. As hard as he'd tried, he wasn't good, and that was all there was to it. He had become popular and cool after he and Ms. M had solved the body in the butter churn murder, but everyone soon forgot about his role in it—except for his mother who made it one more item on her list of things to worry about. Although the idea of being a super hero was still appealing, he had grown up enough to realize that it was only a fantasy. For the moment, at least, he had nothing to replace it. When adults asked him what he wanted to be when he grew up, he shrugged and turned silent. A detective? There might never be another murder in his vicinity. Then what? He might have as dull a job as Ms. M's son, Sheriff Stuart Mulholland, seemed to have.

All that spring, a stream of community leaders had come to talk to Alex's class, each about his or her career. Sheriff Mulholland's talk had been a real drag. He'd explained that his work was nothing like that done by Hawaii Five-O, and then he'd doubled down by delivering the dullest talk of many dull talks. How had Ms. M managed to raise such a boring man? Alex wondered.

On the last day of school Bob Early was on the agenda. He was a youthful older guy who owned one of the biggest car lots in the Northeast Kingdom. He dressed like a casual millionaire, or the way Alex thought a casual millionaire would dress—tieless, gray sports coat, blue slacks. "Hi," he said to them, sitting on the edge of a desk. "I'm Bob Early. I'm a used car salesman." They all laughed, even though car salesman jokes weren't part of their life experience.

Women probably thought he was cute, Alex guessed. He had one of those boyish faces with dimples. Alex had one too, but he hoped it would go away by the time he started shaving. Bob Early looked like a guy who worked out: he was still muscled, even though he was probably older than he looked. Maybe as old as Ms. M. He didn't have a paunch. He smiled a lot which, Alex was sure, was the way you tried to sell stuff. It probably made him a little bit of a phony. Still, cars and money were good things.

Mr. Early went on to explain that he sold both used and new cars, and that he loved his work. He told them obscure nothing facts about buying the best used cars in Florida where the weather was mild and the cars had no rust; about the pricing of automobiles used and new; about the excitement of getting brand-new cars on the lot and finding the right customers for them. Someone asked him how long it had taken him to build up a business as big as his.

"It's been a few decades, but we've never done badly. We're good. I have a crackerjack team of salesmen. I buy the best and I sell the best. I have an excellent utterly professional money manager I'd trust with my life. She's also my sister-in-law, so I have to be complimentary," he added, laughing.

What course of study would he recommend for kids interested in pursuing a career in the automobile sales business? "Some math, some science, a little of everything. You have to know how to talk; you have to like people. It helps to understand how an automobile works! Mostly, just a little bit of everything."

Everyone applauded heartily.

When Bob Early left, Alex watched him from the window. His smile had disappeared; he looked worried. Alex, being Alex, wondered about what. He'd figured out some time ago that happy adults were usually pretending. Bob Early almost certainly had been doing just that. Except for his mother and Ms. M, all the adults he knew were hypocritical about almost everything.

V

On spring cleanup day, the museum grounds teemed with volunteers raking leaves, cleaning out flower beds, planting pansies around the Cyril Benning House, and pruning away the gray twisted branches that stretched out from trees and bushes like foreign appendages grown over the winter. Alex and Coker worked on the pond with their favorite volunteer, Nick Craft, moving heaps of sodden leaves, trying to clear the water of the algae that would paint it a slimy green this summer, turn the edges to sludge, and make it hard for the fish who lived there to thrive.

Alex had cleared the dock area of leaves. He was raking underneath it, thrusting his rake into the dark water and pulling out debris, when he caught onto something bigger and heavier. Very slowly, tugging until he almost fell in, he combed the rough surface under the water until he dragged out what looked like an overcoat with big copper buttons. "What the devil," he muttered. But he knew what it was. "I've hooked the coat of the phantom organist," he said to himself. "There's a body down there." He could feel his head getting light, his hands trembling, and an odd quivering covering him like a fit. Why did things like this happen to him? Alex, the gutless wonder. Detectives on TV programs found dead bodies all the time, and their most troubled reaction was a grimace.

He sank down onto the dock and thought about what he should do. Should he alert Nick, or get Coker over to help him? Nick had gone for a coffee break with Lori. Coker was whistling a tuneless song, working the opposite shore. Ms. Mulholland would know, he thought to himself, and she would want to know about his find right away.

He found her spading the earth for pansies, chattering to his mother and Cornelia Early. He stooped down and murmured breathlessly into her ear. "I think I've found a body. I think it's the organist."

"Oh, my!" said Ms. Mulholland. "Did you say what

I thought you said?"

He nodded solemnly.

"I'll be right back," she told the women. "Alex has found something in the pond he needs advice about." She followed him across the road and down to the dock.

The coat looked like a drowned animal— bedraggled, sopping wet, limp. She studied it quietly. "There's more of something down there?" she asked Alex. He nodded numbly. "Stuart would have my head," she said as she rifled through the pockets and, startled at what she found, secreted it away in her own pocket.

"Where's Nick?" she asked.

"Having coffee with Lori up by the Education Center."

"Can you go get him without letting Lori know anything's wrong?"

Alex nodded and set off at a run while Ms. Mulholland sat on the deck quietly, thinking about where a body would have to fall to end up under the dock. After all, it wasn't necessarily murder. The man could have been drunk and stumbled into the pond, although he would have had to be very drunk indeed. The water was no more than three or four feet deep. He might have had a heart attack. A possibility, if an odd one. What was he doing down here in the first place? There was no organ here. No globe to scribble poetry on. Just two other mysterious people, one of them worried about going to prison.

What if he'd been killed somewhere else and the body deposited under the dock? It wouldn't have been impossible to put him there. If Alex hadn't been so thorough, the man could have stayed there undiscovered until the summer sun warmed the pond enough for real decay to set in.

Alex could be wrong. There might be nothing more there. Just muck and weeds. The organist could have tired of his overcoat and thrown it into the water. Not likely.

Nick came striding across the grass and down the hill to where she sat: "What's up, Tasha?"

"I want you to bring up whatever's under the dock without calling anyone's attention to what's happening here."

The Organist Who Wore Gloves

"A public relations disaster if Alex is right."

"Yes. Dead bodies do make for that sort of thing."

Still shaking, Alex sat down on the grassy bank above the pond and watched Nick pull on a pair of hip boots. What kind of detective am I? he thought—I should be looking for evidence, not just sitting here. He studied the ground around him. That was when he spotted a cigarette butt in the grass. He picked it up carefully, and stuck it in his jacket pocket. Definitely evidence. A Camel.

Nick smiled at him grimly and waded into the murky water. With Alex's rake, he gently prodded and pulled, then drew something to the near surface. A gloved hand.

"I'm sorry," he said. "We'd better get the police."

Tasha nodded. "I'll go call them," she said. "Don't do more. They may have ways of doing less damage to the body. Just sort of stand guard over the dock, will you? Tell anyone who asks as little as possible. Alex, you'd better go talk to Coker. He's suffering a slow death from curiosity." She reddened a little—the expression seemed indelicate under the circumstances.

"My God, what is it with this place?" asked Sheriff Stuart Mulholland, staring down at the body. "Murder almost never happens in this town. Doesn't anyone here know that?"

"I'm sure this is entirely coincidental, Stuart. You can tell people that, can't you? The victim is someone who has nothing to do with the Shrubsbury Museum. Someone just left a body here."

"Certainly," said Lori. "No one knows this man. His murder has nothing to do with this museum."

"We don't know that he was murdered, Lori. He could have had a stroke or a heart attack, fallen in and drowned."

"Maybe Agatha Hamilton's death made someone think that this is a logical place to leave bodies," muttered Winifred Persinger, the president of the board, wondering how her interest in history had led to this, and beginning to plan her escape to some less dismal form of community service.

Serendipity Hamilton, the daughter of the deceased Agatha Hamilton, alarmed by all the commotion, wandered out of the neighboring Hamilton House in a great purple dressing gown and moved regally among them. "Very strange. Very strange. I don't recognize him at all. I wouldn't recognize him even if he hadn't turned white and blubbery. Poor, poor man."

VI

The next week after the murder was eerie and quiet even though school was out. Kids were discouraged from coming around by their parents, but while the museum wouldn't open officially until the following Sunday, tourists pulled up on the road by the pond and stared down at the dock. Lori explained again and again that there was no connection between the corpse and the museum. Sometimes an early volunteer would take up the litany. Alex's mother wasn't so sure, and kept him home after school. One murder had been enough. She couldn't believe there was another. She thought about moving somewhere tropical; she was sick of winter in the North Country. Maybe a small warm town in Florida with no crime. The sheriff hadn't found any identification on the body in the pond, and no one claimed him. The coroner determined that he'd been shot with a small caliber pistol, but the information was kept quiet in the hope that it would help in the investigation.

More than ever Tasha kept to herself. She worked in the flowerbeds; she trimmed the bushes around the Cyril Benning and Timothy Evensong houses. If anyone had been watching her—but no one was—they would have noticed that she stopped working time and again to gaze thoughtfully into space, and that she sometimes pulled something from her front shirt pocket and studied it. She played the cello more frequently than usual. She wrote letters, but no one knew to whom or about what and no one was interested enough to ask.

On a late afternoon a few days after the body was discovered, she and her dog, Gusty, were wandering in the cemetery when Alex and Coker sped up on their bicycles. "I'm not supposed to be here," Alex said breathlessly.

"Me neither," said Coker.

"Do you know anything yet, Ms. M?"

"Not much, boys. I think we'd better sit this one out, though. Your parents are really upset."

"Oh, come on. You know you can't do anything without me. I already know things you don't, and I know you know things I don't." Alex knelt down beside Gusty and scratched him behind both floppy ears. The dog licked his face and pushed him down to make a tumbling heap of boy and dog.

Ms. M laughed. "So what is it I don't know, Alex?" she asked, hoping against hope for something, anything helpful.

"I think I know who the woman was," he said, rolling out from under Gusty.

"Oh, Alex, that's major. I hope you haven't told anyone. It could be dangerous."

"Only Coker."

"Thank God. So tell me now. Who?"

"Not unless you tell what you know. You took something out of the dead guy's overcoat pocket. What was it?"

"Let's go somewhere where no one can see or hear us. Okay, guys?"

They made their way to the back of the graveyard

where shrubbery had grown up around a grave so that it was no longer visible; the stone had fallen and lay there like a conference table waiting for business to be discussed, papers to be signed, reports made. It was the perfect secret meeting place. "The caretakers don't even seem to know this is here," Ms. M said with a sad smile. "The family moved away long ago and no one has kept watch."

"Who's first?" asked Coker.

"I'll show you what I found," Ms. M said, and reached into her pocket. "It's not much, and I don't know if it will ever be of help to us. I've kept silent about it because I think the world at large will take it to mean something it probably doesn't."

She pulled out an old skeleton key that looked like the one that opened the front door of the museum. It was on a chain with a medallion of an organ.

"You mean everyone will think his death has to do with the museum?"

"Yes. And since none of us knows who he is, I'm fairly certain it doesn't."

"He was hanging around."

"Yes. He was that. But we haven't a clue why. The police haven't been able to identify him."

"It looks like the other old keys," said Coker, tracing its pattern. "Not like someone copied it."

"It does, doesn't it? Like he had it forever. And now, Alex, it's your turn. Who do you think it was?"

"You're gonna be surprised and you're not going to believe me," Alex warned. Ms. M shrugged her shoulders. "Who Alex?"

"I'm not absolutely sure but it sounded like Mrs. Early."

"In the name of all that's holy—that's next to impossible. How could it be her?" sputtered Ms. M.

"I told you she'd say that," Alex said to Coker.

"She's a respectable woman from an old and respectable family. She's our volunteer treasurer at the museum. She's the financial officer and accountant for Early's Auto, the oldest and most profitable business in the area. She plays the piano for the church choir. And besides all that, she's a nice woman."

"I told you she'd say that too," Alex sighed. "I can't

help it, Ms. M. That's who it sounded like."

"I don't know what to do with your information, Alex. I can't outright ask her if she was at the pond in the middle of the night where the murdered man was found a few nights after, arguing with someone and swearing that she would not go to prison. Now can I?"

"I guess not. You could just choose not to believe me," Alex said, annoyed.

"No, I can't. That's the problem. Mrs. Early's voice is very distinctive. It would be difficult for you to mistake her for anyone else."

"Maybe you can be subtle," suggested Coker. "Trick her. Get her to admit to being there without her ever knowing you know something."

"I can try, Coker, but I really don't know how. Easier said than done."

"You'll let us know after you try, won't you?" asked Alex. "What would you like us to do?"

"I wish I knew, Alex. I'm stymied, I'm afraid. I did have one thought. The phantom organist always rode a bicycle here, didn't he? It sounded like a gearless rattletrap. I wondered if you guys could look for it. If we could figure out where he got it, we might have a lead. Or look for someone who recognizes it. I told Stuart that we'd heard a bicycle being ridden off in the middle of the night and he might want to look for it, but he hasn't done anything about it as far as I know. The man has no respect for my intelligence, I'm afraid. Something about the way I raised him, I guess."

"We're on it, Ms. M," Alex said. "Don't worry. Between you and us, we'll figure it out."

Alex and Coker gathered up their bicycles and set off down the road. "Something's wrong," Alex said. "She's not acting right."

"What do you mean? She seemed pretty normal to me. She was nice. She was surprised by Mrs. Early. Is that what you mean?"

"Nah, something else is wrong. That organist meant a lot to her, and I don't know why. I mean, he wasn't even that good, at least not on the Estey."

"A fellow musician. That might be all it is, Alex. If I lost one of the Beastie Boys, I'd be pretty messed up about it."

"No. She's all bent out of shape, and I don't know why. She isn't talking to me the way she used to."

"She doesn't want to upset your mother."

"Yeah, I guess. You wanna start looking for the bike here? This is about the distance he ran before we heard him rolling away."

"Yeah, why don't you go that way and I'll go this, maybe a hundred or so feet, and when we meet back in the middle we'll do the same again, further from the road?"

"Yep," said Alex. He scanned the underbrush, still brown and broken from the winter, sometimes ducking into bushes as tall as he was. He didn't understand why, but he was deeply unhappy about this murder. His old partner was telling him scarcely anything. His mother was on his case. Coker every now and again seemed like a terrible dunderhead.

Maybe he and Ms. M were just growing apart. Maybe his hormones were out of control and she didn't know how to talk to him anymore. More likely, she was the problem, though. Not him. She seemed distant and distracted. Like she was mourning the guy. Jeeze, she didn't even know him, and besides there was no proof he was some kind of brain. So he remembered some poetry. He may have brought the book with him. Who knew? Why did she care so much? And why wouldn't she talk about it to him?

He and Coker met in the middle, exchanged some desultory remarks, and started off again. Alex was in despair. Coker didn't have enough imagination for this job; he didn't know things like Ms. M did, but somehow, ever since they'd slept over in the museum, Coker had become his partner. He missed Ms. M. He couldn't say anything to anyone. Not to Coker, of course. Certainly not to his mother—she wanted him to stay away from the museum. His friends, to a man, would wonder what was wrong with him, worrying about an old lady who wasn't even his grandma.

"Hey, Alex! I think I've found the place where it was!"

Alex tracked Coker to where there had been a bike at the end of a broken path. They followed the path back to the road. "Someone rode it away. Or, took it away," said Coker.

"Yeah. I wonder if it was the sheriff."

"Ms. M said, 'No.'"

"Yeah. Maybe whoever did him in, huh? Let's go over the track again. Maybe, someone's accidentally left something."

They studied the brush, the matted grass and the muddy track. That was how they found another cigarette stub. A Camel, not more than a few days old.

VII

When Tasha left the graveyard with Gusty and went upstairs to her apartment she took up her cello and began to play. She'd hoped for a blinding insight, a revelation. But she was as confused as Alex, though not about the same things.

From the first, she'd cared about the organist, although she couldn't say why. Something about what he was doing touched her. The music, of course. The poem. But it went deeper than that. And after they found his body, it was worse.

Alex was right that she wasn't telling everything she knew. She hadn't recognized the dead man, but she had recognized the key. It had belonged to her late husband. She had no idea why his key had shown up in another man's pocket or, especially, why that man was dead.

The Organist Who Wore Gloves

She'd stopped caring about her ex long ago, way before he died when he tumbled from a catwalk at the Estey organ factory in Brattleboro. Her son, the sheriff, had claimed to be even less interested, but considering he'd been a toddler when his father left, she'd never believed him. She wasn't going to remind him of his father's departure now. Perhaps the key had been discarded somewhere, and retrieved by the organist who harbored a fondness for old places with organs. Perhaps it had nothing to do with Sheriff Stuart Mulholland's father. Perhaps.... but whatever she came up with seemed unlikely, no matter how she tried to explain it, with or without the presence of her long-gone husband. There was no story she could tell herself that made it make sense. She felt as if she were struggling with too many stories, sad tales from the past and absurd tales from the present day—being taken in by an undertow, a riptide, a watery vortex pulling her under along with that sad, white body.

Well, perhaps it wasn't all quite that melodramatic.

However, her ex-husband's part in it, whatever it was, made it especially troubling. It brought back bad memories, bad feelings, lost hopes....

She'd been thirty-two when he'd had his affair, and thirty-three when he left. She'd kept track of him, not because she wanted him back but because she thought Stuart deserved a father. He'd sent checks the first two months, and then nothing. Not even a letter. Another month and he was dead and that was that.

Now, all these years later his key to the museum and a medallion she'd never seen before turned up in the pocket of a man shot and thrown into the farm pond across the road. It was frightening. Not because it meant Max was back in her life, but because it made no sense.

VIII

Ms. M had greeted the news of the bike tracks without enthusiasm, and Alex left her that day, swearing to solve the crime himself. He didn't need her; he had never needed her. He'd figure the whole thing out without her.

It was entirely possible that he didn't have his job anymore. Ms. M didn't seem to care and his mother was glad to have him stay home. But he knew how to work around them. He asked Lori whether he could make a few dollars cleaning up the cluster flies that had accumulated with the warmer temperatures. Lori raised her eyebrows: "I should say so. Tasha shouldn't have to do it, and no one else is willing. If your mother asks, I'll just say I forgot she didn't want you working here. You offered and we were terribly grateful. You're a hard worker and always so thorough, so I said, "'Get to work.' And you did."

He'd worked his way down from the fourth floor to the first, brushing the dead and the dying flies into a bucket where their black bodies rattled together, and the survivors still buzzed. They were disgusting, and some of them didn't want to die and tried to get away. But he had no empathy for flies. He was cold-blooded. He was a detective. He checked out everything in one room and then another, hoping to make a new discovery. By the time he got to the music room he had almost given up. He hadn't found the remotest kind of clue.

Leaving the organ until last, he did the windows quickly: the music room was sheltered from the sun and there were far fewer flies here than upstairs. Finally, he examined the organ. He looked in the bench where the music was kept—a few old hymn books, some music for popular songs of the early twentieth century. That was about it except for an even older book called *The Sweet Touch, Organ Solos for the Beginning Student.* He'd looked through its yellowing pages before and wondered aloud that anyone any time could be inspired by it. Ms. M had laughed and agreed.

The Organist Who Wore Gloves

He was about to put it back in its place when, perhaps on a detective's hunch, he opened the cover. There were still yellow pages, but there were also checks. Just a few, all of them recent, made out to an account at the Pioneer Bank and signed by Cornelia Early. Some of them were for large amounts.

"I'd like to show you the kitchen, Zoe. We need someone to act the role of a cook now and again, and I think you'd be perfect." It was Mrs. Early showing one of the new student interns around the building. He closed the book and the top of the organ bench abruptly, sank to his knees and began rubbing down the carpeted pedals. "Excuse me," he said to Cornelia Early and the intern. "Someone seems to have muddied them and I'm cleaning them up."

"Of course," said Mrs. Early. "Zoe, I want you to meet Alex Churchill. He works here off and on."

"Hi," said Alex, struggling to his feet. "Hi," said Zoe. Oh jeeze, he thought. She was astonishing. Her sweater was tight, his mother would have said much too tight. He could almost feel her breasts with his fingertips. Her hair had been brushed many times and her lips were a perfect bow. She was the most beautiful girl he'd ever seen. His cheeks were hot and he felt like a fool.

Generally, girls were still more of a puzzle than a subject of interest to him, but there were moments like this when the sudden sight of one could leave him feeling set loose from every mooring, free floating, lost. He was conscious that his body was changing. He couldn't keep up with it.

He trailed them into the kitchen, dusting every windowsill, trying not to look at the girl. Or for that matter, at Mrs. Early. He had to get the book out and to Ms. M before the woman worried that he'd seen it and retrieved it. Of that he was sure. He knew whose voice he'd heard that night. He knew who'd given him an odd look when she came into the music room, and who, even now, was watching him carefully.

He didn't know whether to be glad when Ms. M walked through the kitchen door. "Alex! Cornelia! Just the people I wanted to see."

"Alex, your mother telephoned. I told her I'd search you out if you were here. She'd like you home immediately or sooner. So scoot!"

"Cornelia, Lori wants to see you. Says she has some questions about the cost breakdown for our interns this year. I can take over for you with Zoe if you'd like."

The Organist Who Wore Gloves

"Of course, Tasha. Zoe, I leave you in the capable hands of Ms. Mulholland." The woman walked to the kitchen door and looked back at Alex. "Coming, Alex?"

"I think I left something upstairs," Alex said. "In a minute."

Cornelia Early left and Alex headed to the music room. "Ms. M," he called to her, "could you take a look at something in here? See if I cleaned up the pedals okay?"

Tasha smiled at Zoe and signaled to her to wait a moment. Standing in the doorway, looking at Alex, her eyes wide when she saw the bench open, she walked over and looked down, studying the open music book, and shaking her head. She nodded at him, picked up the book and handed it to him. "Hide it in the closet," she said softly. "Under the flags in the bottom drawer."

"Take care, Alex. If your mom's too upset, have her call me. Be in touch."

"Thanks, Ms. M," he said. But he worried when he saw Mrs. Early watching him from the second floor of the Timothy Evensong House. He worried all evening. But what in the name of all that was holy could he do about it?

Tasha locked both the front and the kitchen doors carefully when she left with an armful of flags. They needed to be refreshed periodically and she was the only one who remembered and carefully cleaned them every year. Once in her apartment, however, she tossed the flags onto the couch in an unpatriotic heap. She was more interested in what Alex had found in the organ bench.

She sat down at her desk with the old music book at its center, opened it and stared in wonder at the checks. "Cornelia, Cornelia," she murmured. "What have you been doing?"

The checks were made out to a "doing business as" account in the name of Early's Auto. Worth thousands of dollars, they were not only signed by Cornelia, they were endorsed by her. But why were they hidden in the organ bench? Maybe they weren't meant to be hidden. Perhaps they'd just been placed here because she had some overtime to do one day while she waited to guide a tour, and it seemed like a secure place to put them. But wouldn't she have retrieved them as soon as possible and put them back where they belonged? What if there were more? Cornelia had worked as the bookkeeper at Early's Motors for at least thirty years.

The Organist Who Wore Gloves

Thirty years of bookkeeping.

Thirty years of embezzlement?

Tasha hadn't forgotten that Alex had heard a woman worrying about prison in Cornelia's voice. Was this why she was worried? Had Cornelia been writing herself checks while she and her husband, Colin, raised their children and built their house and took vacations they shouldn't have had the money for but apparently had? And what should she, Tasha Mulholland, do about it? She couldn't accuse the woman of a crime if she wasn't sure. And what if it had something to do with the murder? And who was the organist and why did he know Cornelia? Who was the other man?

The next morning, at about the same time local farmers got up to milk, before anyone else was up, Tasha took Cornelia Early's checks and copied them. Then she took the music book with its odd contents across the greensward to the museum and put it back in the organ bench, under the other music—she assumed that that was where it had been, it had always been there, even when it was just music.

That was the same morning the *Burlington Free Press* declared in a feature story about murder in

Shrubsbury that the crime, supposing it was one, almost certainly had nothing to do with the museum. Poor Shrubsbury and its history museum were getting a bum rap. It was likely that someone with a perverse idea of where to put a dead body had left it in the pond. As far as the newspaper was concerned, the museum and the town deserved clean bills of health.

Alex came to work after school that day. Ms. M was glad to see him. He was nearly ecstatic about his latest success as a detective. He tried not to think what his mother would do when she found out that the dead man was a phantom who played the organ in the museum. He'd cross that bridge when he came to it. In the meantime, he wanted to fix whatever was wrong with Ms. M.

IX

Cornelia Early was frightened. She'd retrieved the checks from the organ bench, and returned them to her office at home. That was two days ago, and she was still worried that Alex and Tasha Mulholland had seen them. Something seemed not quite right with the way the old music book lay in the organ bench, as if someone had rummaged around, someone like Alex. He'd been right there, almost hiding at the base of the organ when she came in with Zoe. He'd been clumsy, red-faced, fidgety. Even taking into account Zoe's tight, tight sweater....

The girl had been flattered. She thought Alex's bluster was all about her. Cornelia prayed that she was right.

Granted, Alex and Tasha might be trying to find

something that would link the body in the pond with the museum. The checks wouldn't have done that. But if they'd spotted them they would have wondered, at the very least, why they were there. If they'd studied them, they might have begun to figure it out.

Tasha had rushed in on her way to Brattleboro that morning, God knows for what purpose, but she took the boy with her. She'd smiled at Cornelia and brewed her a cup of one of her own special coffees. She'd chattered about the weather and the Estey Organ Company. It was clear she knew something or she wouldn't be going to Brattleboro of all places. Still, Brattleboro had nothing to do with Cornelia's predicament. At least not directly.

No, it was best to hope that the nosy pair had never seen the checks. They hadn't had any reason to look into the old music book, or even to open the bench, and Tasha had certainly been herself this morning. The same eager old lady out to have another adventure. She hadn't looked at Cornelia as if she were anyone but the dear friend she'd known for years and years.

Cornelia had grown up in Shrubsbury. Even at sixty-something she was almost beautiful, and men in their forties had been heard to say she was hot. Her face was striking, but not really attractive. Her eyes were wide and such an unusual shade of blue no one noticed that her lips were thin and her chin weak. Although her manner was gentle and soft, and her demeanor almost shy, there was something about her that was deeply, surprisingly sexual.

She'd been courted when she was young by many young men, even by Max Mulholland, though she would never have said anything to Tasha about it—they had been teenagers. The Early brothers had both wooed her. Colin had won out, possibly because he was the handsomest of the brothers, and he and Cornelia had been married when he returned to the area after graduating from the University of Vermont. They'd raised two children who were grown and living far away. Bob Early, the short, baby-faced brother, married very late. From his family's point of view, his morose, bad-tempered wife, Adele, had not been a good choice.

Cornelia went outside and paced, sipping her Bright Morning coffee when she reached the raspberry patch, then turning around to walk to the juniper that overlooked the pond. She stopped and stared down at it. Lord knows, she wasn't really to blame for what had happened, but she was sorry. Tasha waved at her as she and Alex drove away in the yellow truck.

Alex's mother had seemed pleased when Tasha Mulholland asked if she could take him with her on a trip to the museum in Brattleboro. He'd be out of what still seemed like a pernicious environment; he'd be visiting another museum far away with his might-as-well-be adopted grandmother. They'd be thinking about something besides murder.

"So now you're going to tell me everything, Ms. M," Alex said, tugging on his seat belt. "Okay?"

"Certainly most of it, Alex," she replied with her old smile, the smile he'd worried she'd lost.

"All of it," he declared happily, settling into the passenger's seat of the yellow truck.

"Remember the key that I found in the organist's coat pocket?"

"Yep. And the medallion."

"The medallion is one of the things we want to explore today."

The Organist Who Wore Gloves

"Because it's an organ?"

"Uh huh. Partly. But the key is the really interesting thing."

"Why?"

"Because it's the key that belonged to my husband."

"Your husband? I guess I knew you had one once. But why did he have a key to the museum? He died, didn't he?"

"Yes, many years ago now. Decades. When we came to Shrubsbury, we became museum caretakers to help pay the bills. He'd had a long history in Shrubsbury as a boy and everyone was glad he wanted the responsibility. There was no director then. There was nobody except for a few board members who didn't do much of anything except meet every few weeks."

"When he left you got the job full time?"

"Not exactly. A few years later. Anyway, Max, my husband, had the keys to the building then, and he absentmindedly left with them. The other key on the ring was like most keys, but the front door key was special, of course. And this one is even more special than the others. Unlike the others, it has an inscription on it. It says, 'Open door.' Rather, odd, I always thought. What else would you do with a key?"

"So you know it's the same one."

"That's right."

"Why are we going to Brattleboro?"

"That's where the Estey organ was produced. That's where Max went when he left, and where he died a few months later."

"Oh wow. That's crazy. How did he die?"

"He fell off a catwalk into a mess of organ pipes at the Estey factory."

"Jeeze. I'm sorry, Ms. M."

"Remember, it's a very long time ago," she said, smiling at him.

"What was he doing at the Estey factory?"

"I don't know. I didn't feel I should try to find out. He'd already remarried."

"Boy! What a jerk!"

Tasha laughed out loud. "Thank you, Alex. You do

my heart good."

Alex grinned. "But really, Ms. M. What do you hope to find out? Did someone push him off the catwalk?"

"I don't know. I think it's unlikely he was murdered. He wasn't the kind of man to get murdered, not that that makes any sense."

"Are you sure he's dead?"

"He has to be. His son and I lived in Shrubsbury, not that far distant. He cared about Stuart. He wouldn't have ignored his son's existence."

"That's right. He was the sheriff's dad."

"Yes. I know that seems odd to you. Stuart's a mature man."

"And a sheriff."

"And a sheriff."

"So who are we talking to? Are we looking for the medallion?"

"We're going to talk to someone who knew Max back then. I don't know how well. And we're checking to see if the Estey people ever produced medallions like that one, or if they recognize it. And, of course, we're going to the factory, or what was the factory."

"What are you going to do about Mrs. Early?"

"I think I had better talk to her before I do anything. I can't just blithely warn her I may have the evidence to send her to prison. I have to let her know I know that she may have done something. I couldn't tell that much from the checks. But she's been at Early's Motors for thirty or more years. I can't imagine what everyone would think if she really were guilty of something. When we get back I'll arrange to spend some time with her."

"You'll be careful, won't you, Ms. M? I mean she might be a criminal. No matter how nice she seems." Alex had decided to play the man's role; he'd take care of his elderly partner, even if he didn't always understand what she was going through. Many women were betrayed by their husbands and left with small boys. He was a case in point. His father had been a pretty terrible guy, it seemed to him. Ms. M's husband hadn't been much better.

But mostly, the trip was awesome. There they were,

on the road together, on the case, and worrying about each other. The detectives no criminal would ever worry about. The harmless old lady and the excitable kid.

The yellow truck took to the road as if it had been up and down Interstate 91 many times—over the long lounging hills, singing down the highway that stretched through forests, overlooked farmland, and scaled hillsides and cliffs above the winding, glinting ribbon of the Connecticut River. Below them was fallow farmland, rich and dark, checkered by yellowing fields of mustard greens and alfalfa and rye in nearly as many shades of green as there were acres. There were forests still veiled in young growth, translucent, almost metallic when the sun shone on them from the right angle.

They stopped at overlooks and looked through binoculars at ospreys and eagles. They counted boats meandering down the river. Now and again, they wandered down to the river valley floor and looked for ice cream and collectibles.

Ms. M turned somber when they rolled into Brattleboro. Alex knew why without really understanding anything. Grown-up dramas. But even though he'd never been in love, he knew it must hurt for someone to cheat and leave, and that she must still be hurt by it. Even after more years than he could conceive. Thirty, forty. He had weeks to wait for year thirteen, and that seemed an eternity. Both Alex and Ms. M realized all over again how very young he was—or how very old she was.

X

To Alex, Brattleboro was almost a city. His experience with towns of any size was limited, but he knew bookstores, art galleries and restaurants were awesome. He knew that movie houses and exercise clubs were even more important. He'd watched cool young men on television. He longed to walk the town's streets and hear people greeting each other since, watching from the truck, they all seemed to know each other, and a lot of them seemed young, not as young as he was, of course, but what he would be soon.

They found what was left of the factory, seven long three-story buildings—the seventh had been joined to the eighth to make one. On the middle building was a large round clock, like a giant pocket watch. That was where they found the Estey museum, a tall, wide room with organs scattered around it, and where they met the old man who had once been a factory manager.

Gerald Must's snappy pin-striped gray suit hung on his narrow shoulders the way it must have hung on the hanger a few hours before, elegant and expensive, but unflattering. He came into the room slowly—the suit following him, his slender frame wavering. He had a cane in one hand, and he grasped the door frame with the other, while he anxiously searched for a chair with his rheumy eyes. He kissed Tasha's hand, and shook Alex's hand gravely.

"So you're Tasha Mulholland," he said, squinting at her.

"Yes. Am I a surprise?"

"That you're here at all is a surprise. Otherwise, no, not really. Max said you were a handsome woman, strong, stronger than he was. Is this young man your grandson?"

"No, Max's son Stuart married, but so far there haven't been any children. Alex is a friend."

"And you never married again?"

"No."

The Organist Who Wore Gloves

"But of course that's none of my business."

Their voices were tight and tense. Why were they already angry when they'd only just started talking to each other, Alex wondered. It wasn't like Ms. M not to exude warmth and kindliness. And this old guy—he didn't even know her and he seemed to hate her.

"No, it's not. At any rate, it hasn't anything to do with why I'm here. When Max left Shrubsbury, he took a key with him, a large skeleton key like this one." She pulled it out of her purse. "I assumed at the time that he'd just forgotten to leave it."

"Quite a key," murmured Gerald Must.

"You've never seen it before?"

"No. Should I have?"

"I don't know, Mr. Must. The key and a medal that I think might be from here were the only objects on a key chain in the coat pocket of a man found dead in the pond at the Old Shrubsbury School Museum less than a week ago."

"Extraordinary," said Gerald Must.

"I think so. Especially since the medal was this

medallion of an old pedal organ." She handed it to him.

"It's an Estey, all right. It's the one right over there," he said pointing somewhere across the room with a wavering finger.

"Were a bunch of these medals made sometime during the history of the company? When? And are they still turning up?"

"Yes, they were made at its end. Someone, I don't recall who, had some made in an effort to raise morale."

"I assume we're talking about 1960, '61."

"Yes." He was fingering the medallion, reminiscing, Alex thought. "I haven't seen one in many years," he said.

"But Max could have gotten hold of one then."

"Yes. And probably did. But I don't know what that has to do with your drowned man."

"Nor do I. But I have a photograph. Do you recognize him?" Ms. M pulled out a 4" x 5" of the drowned man. Alex hadn't seen it before; he'd only seen the body itself from a distance. He studied Gerald Must as the man took the snapshot from Ms. M and looked at it closely. Alex thought he saw his face pale but he was already ashen so he couldn't be certain. The hand that held the picture trembled. It could have been because it was a picture of a dead person, but Alex guessed Gerald Must recognized the organ player.

"I've never seen him before," he answered.

"The key chain was in a camel's hair coat pocket," Ms. Mulholland said helpfully.

"He's just not familiar," the man said quietly and looked straight at her. His gaze was steady even if nothing else about him was.

"I'm afraid I'm not of much assistance." He smiled, glad, Alex thought, and not at all sorry to be of no help.

"I have another set of questions," Ms. Mulholland said, returning his smile with a dim one of her own.

"I'll do what I can," the old man replied.

"How did Max die?"

"You never inquired then, did you? Why are you asking now?"

"He'd left me a few months before. His new wife told me that he'd been glad to be rid of me. She preferred that I not make any inquiries, and that I stay away from the services. I wasn't needed or wanted for anything."

"Belinda."

"I guess that was her name."

"Belinda was a very possessive woman. She took charge of all the arrangements. As soon as the funeral was over, she left town."

"Is she still alive?"

"As a matter of fact, she died recently. They'd moved to Virginia and I hadn't heard from her in years."

"They?"

"She had a child."

"How do you know she died?"

"Can't remember. Old age, you know. It was a few weeks ago. I just can't remember who...."

"And how did Max die?" she asked abruptly. Ms. M had turned gray and gaunt. Alex hoped she'd be finished with this awful man soon.

"He was in the factory. We were trying to put new emphasis on electronic organs then, and he had grand ideas about promoting the instruments. The rest of us—myself, Belinda, Noah Patrovsky, one of the designers, Leonard—were here in this office. We heard a rumble and the crash of pipes. It was clear that some of the biggest and heaviest had fallen, and when we went to see what had happened we discovered that Max had fallen into a pipe organ. It was a curious way to die. I think he would have laughed about it."

"Were you able to talk to him before he died?" Ms. M asked, with a sharp intake of breath.

"Yes. But he didn't say anything that would pertain to you, then or now."

"What did he say?"

"Just told us Belinda was pregnant and to see to her."

"That's it?"

"That was it. He didn't mention you. Why should he have? He was only just conscious."

"So Max had a child with Belinda."

"Yes. I suppose that means the boy is a year or two younger than your son."

"And he was born in Virginia?"

"Yes."

"And you've never seen him since?"

"No. I must stop now, Ms. Mulholland. I'm not well. I haven't anything else to say."

"Thank you, Mr. Must. I wish you could think of someone else who might know something."

"Sorry. Can't." His voice had gotten raspy and breathless. "Get my wife. Please. She's outside in the gray car."

"We'll send her in," Tasha said, almost gruffly, and not at all sympathetically. She walked out of the room at a fast clip, with Alex trailing after.

XI

"He lied. Did you hear him, Alex? He lied more than once," said Ms. Mulholland, grimly twisting straws into grotesque figures, ignoring her cocoa. "He's sickly, but that's no excuse."

"Isn't there anyone else we could talk to?" asked Alex.

"No one. Can you believe he holds a grudge against me because I was the ex? The only other person I knew to try and talk to pleaded near-death and said he couldn't make it." She sighed a great sigh. "I've gotten copies of Max's obituary and a news item about his death. But I don't know where Belinda went. There's only a mention of her and none at all of her son. I don't know where and when she died. I don't know where Max's son is or even his name. I don't know anything more about the medallion. Must told us as little as possible."

Alex had never seen Ms. M quite as upset as this, and he didn't know what to do about it. He was, he reminded himself, only a kid, and an old woman wasn't likely to take too much encouragement from him.

"What do you think he lied about?"

"He recognized the dead man in the picture. Max's death was at the very least more complicated than he described. He's been in touch with Belinda and her son over the years. How's that for a beginning?"

"Did you think he was really as old as he seemed? I don't think he was that old or sick. His wife gave him a kick on the way out."

"Did she? Wasn't she a gruesome woman? You may be right. His face was caked like he'd put on makeup. And all that shaking seemed a bit much. He's probably not much older than I am."

"I think you're right about the dead man's picture," Alex added. "I think he recognized him. So that could mean the phantom organist lived around here some time or other. Maybe he has something to do with Estey organs since he was trying to play one."

"He could have been part of the organ museum; he was too young to have been part of the company."

They brooded over their cocoas, sitting in the restaurant called Amy's Kitchen, Tasha staring unseeing out the window at a grand view of the Connecticut River. She silently wished Alex wasn't with her: she would have dearly loved to be in a bar somewhere with a stiff drink and an older, wiser partner. But while cocoa had nowhere near the clout of whiskey, it warmed and comforted her and gradually she grew calmer. She remembered that she was the adult in charge of this expedition. She remembered to act the adult to Alex's child. She couldn't tell him that she was worried that the dead man was Max's son, and that the very thought made her stomach turn.

Nor did she want to tell her son, the sheriff, that the man he'd been unable to identify could be his half-brother. That she'd taken the key ring from the body would raise Stuart's ire, but she knew he'd forgive it. What bothered her most was that he'd never expressed much curiosity about his father, even though Max leaving had left a hole in his life. Did she have the right to ask him to consider whether the body in the pond was his father's second son when it was only speculation? Would it bring up things in him she didn't know about?

XII

Tasha, at her first opportunity, borrowed Lori's computer and looked for the census records that would name Max's son: Max and Belinda Mulholland and son. Vermont. Virginia. It should have been so easy, but there was no record of a baby Mulholland born on the approximate date in either state. Marriage records for Max and Belinda seemed to be nonexistent. Perhaps they'd never married, but why did Max tell her they had? She looked for Belinda's maiden name, and finally, after three hours and way too much coffee, she located a boy named Max, son of a single woman named Belinda Fox, born in Virginia on a date that was approximate to the one she'd guessed. Max Fox then. Was that the name of the phantom organist who'd been drowned in the pond?

It was surprising how many men named Max Fox lived in the United States: a comedian, a photographer, a businessman, a writer, an electrical worker....

And then there was Cornelia. For the first several days after the trip to Brattleboro, the treasurer was at work and home, and there was no easy way to confront her. When she came back to the museum, Tasha watched the offices in Timothy Evensong's house and waited for a chance, but Lori never left her side, and there seemed to be a stream of people with questions about the struggling finances of the museum. Tasha briefly considered whether Cornelia might have embezzled from the Shrubsbury museum as well as the auto company, but in her head she heard Lori neighing loud and long, asking how Cornelia could ever have squeezed cash, any cash at all, from a turnip.

Finally, Tasha went into the office, ignored the cadre of elderly women who were taking instruction from Cornelia Early about a mailing of requests for donations, and posed her question: "How well did you know Maxwell Fox?" she blurted out.

"I.... I don't know who you're talking about, Tasha."

"The man in the camel overcoat."

"The who? Wait a few minutes, Tasha. I'm almost finished here."

Tasha went outside and sat on the porch steps, gazing across the road at the Shrubsbury Museum, wishing she were somewhere else.

Ten minutes had passed when she saw Cornelia Early drive away in a car that was too new and too nice for someone whose salary was as low as hers.

She ran. As dignified and elderly as Tasha was, she ran to her truck, jumped in, and followed Cornelia down a dirt road that she knew had nothing to do with the road to her house. She was very far behind, and the first junction left her confused, but she took one road rather than another and just kept driving, and there was Cornelia, ahead of her again. There seemed to be no option, just follow the fleeing treasurer anywhere and everywhere until she could face her and ask again: "How well did you know Max Fox? Was Max Fox the man who died in the pond?" It was almost a half hour later when she drove up to Cornelia Early's house, the house that everyone admired with the splendid brickwork in front and the double garage with both doors closed. No one seemed to be at home and she drove off the road into a grove of trees, out of sight, to listen to a Beethoven string quartet on Vermont Public Radio, while she watched the front porch through a lacework of leaves.

"Hey, Ms. Mulholland," said a small voice from the back of the cab.

"Alex! What in the name of all that's holy are you doing here?"

"I caught a ride when you started following Mrs. Early. You're not too angry, are you?"

"No. No, of course not. I've been kind of leaving you out, haven't I?"

"Yep."

"But she mustn't see you. She won't talk if you're here too. You know that."

"Yes. I guess. Although, I am just a kid, remember? She might not pay me much attention."

The quartet was still playing the adagio when Cornelia Early came out onto the porch and looked in both directions, then went back in. A few minutes later, one of the garage doors opened. Tasha gunned her motor and headed for the driveway. "Good move," murmured Alex.

She stopped in the driveway and waited. Would Cornelia back up at full throttle into the yellow truck, or would she try to exit over the lawn? Would she simply give up, sigh and sink back into the plush leather seat, and wait for what was to happen next? It was a standoff.

"I wish she'd make up her mind what she's gonna do. I'm bored," said Alex. "And hungry. You don't have any cookies with you, do you?"

"You shush! We don't want her to hear you."

Almost fifteen minutes passed before Cornelia opened her car door and walked to the yellow truck. She reached up and opened the passenger's door. "Okay," she said in a sad, flat voice. "Ask your questions, Tasha." She pulled herself up and into the truck, and sat there, staring out the window. She looked older than she had the last time Tasha had seen her, only a few hours ago.

"Was Max Fox the man who died in the pond?" Tasha asked.

"I don't know his name," Cornelia responded.

"What do you know? Are you in trouble, Cornelia? I've seen the checks that were hidden in the organ bench."

"I can explain those, Tasha. I know it must look bad."

"You know I might have to tell someone what I know. I'll have to show them the copies I've made."

"Yes. But I want you to wait. We've been friends for a very long time. Give me a chance. I'll tell you everything as soon as I can."

"Was the man who drowned blackmailing you? Was he murdered? Tell me everything."

"Someone has been blackmailing me. I don't know who. And I don't know who the drowned man was."

"Start at the beginning," Tasha said, suddenly feeling sorry for her friend, a kindly soul, a music lover.... Had she really done something seriously wrong? Would she have done something to cheat her employer? She had watched them together. They were genial and fond of each other. Why would she do this to him?

"Please, Tasha. Be patient with me. I'll tell you

everything soon. I'm not a criminal. Truly."

"Oh, Cornelia."

"A couple of months ago, I got a threatening letter from someone who thought, like you, that I was doing something against the law. The sender wanted money, of course."

"What did you do?"

"I thought I might run away, that there might be no other recourse."

"What about confessing all and paying the price?"

"But I'm innocent. And I would hurt so many people."

"Oh, you may already have done that."

"Don't turn me in, Tasha. Not yet. Give me time. Colin and I are trying to make plans. I need to talk to the rest of my family. Please, give me a little time."

"I have no intention of reporting you, Cornelia. You'll have to do that yourself. But I do want to know what your situation has to do with the man who drowned. Alex and his friend Coker camped out in the museum two weeks ago. Alex heard you talking with two gentlemen. Explaining that you didn't want to go to prison. One of those men made a habit of playing the organ in the museum late at night. Who was he? Who was the other man?"

Cornelia was quiet for what seemed a very long time. "I can't tell you anything," she said. In the back of the cab, Alex tensed up, readying himself to jump up with a shout and scare her into telling the truth. "I can't tell you because I honestly don't know who he was. We ran into each other one night at the museum when I was hiding checks and he was writing poetry."

"The other man?"

"He was the organist's friend. He might have been my blackmailer. I could never be sure. But I wasn't sure either one really cared what I was doing around the museum. They didn't want to be exposed any more than I did."

"All this was going on in the dark, icy interior of the museum in the middle of winter. It doesn't make any sense."

"No. I suppose not."

"I don't think you're telling me everything."

"I'm telling you that I really don't know who either man was that night. I never saw any violence. I didn't see what happened to the organist at the pond, I don't even know if it was him. I didn't see the body when you found it. I don't know what any of that was about."

"I don't think I believe you, Cornelia."

"Why would I lie? If I told you everything, you might put in a good word for me. But I have very little to tell."

"Weren't you terribly curious about these men? Didn't you wonder what they were doing in the museum on freezing winter nights?"

"No, truth be told, I only worried that one of them would expose me."

So went the conversation. Alex urged Ms. M on under his breath: She lies. She lies.

"More than ever, Cornelia, I don't believe you. Can't you tell me anything at all?"

"I don't know anything except what you've already heard and seen."

They left it like that. Cornelia wouldn't say more, and Tasha Mulholland didn't know how to make her, not having acquired those sorts of skills, not even having watched the right TV shows. She promised for the time being to say nothing about the checks. Cornelia thanked her profoundly, and promised she wouldn't go anywhere, at least not soon. She left the yellow truck, relieved, while Tasha shook her head in disbelief and something like despair. Alex crawled over the seat and into the place next to her.

"I don't believe her either, Ms. M. I think she knows much more about those two guys than she'll say."

She smiled at the boy. "It's almost dinner time. Why don't I drive you home?" She pulled out of the driveway.

"She's afraid of them, isn't she?" he asked, as she started the drive to Alex's house.

"At least she's afraid of her blackmailer, Alex."

XIII

Alex and Coker met the next morning, bag lunches in their backpacks, to search for the phantom organist's bicycle. Someone had removed the bike; someone who smoked Camels had either ridden it or hauled it away. It was a beat up bike and they could tell from the tracks just where the front tire had been patched. The town of Shrubsbury was a tangle of dirt roads, and more than one yard sported an old gearless bike, but the boys believed that if anyone could find this particular bicycle, they could.

When the organist rode away, he headed west and so the boys did the same, studying farmhouses, barns and outhouses along the way. The day was overcast and the grass and bushes on either side of the road were wet with dew. Here and there, clouds of ground fog hovered over a beaver dam or marsh. They dismounted when they found a muddy driveway with bicycle tire tracks. Coker took out his super sleuth's magnifying glass, and they studied the track together. Nothing. When they reached Shrubsbury Center they found a row of junked bicycles near George Winter's garage.

"Maybe it's one of those," Alex suggested.

"Yeah, but why. Why would someone park a suspicious bike there, where the whole world could see it?"

"Because people like you would ask that question and not bother to look. Did you see *CSI* on TV last week? The killer dude was clever and hid the murder weapon where everyone could see it, so no one did."

Coker sighed and jumped off his bike. "Okay," he said. "Let's go look." He started from one end and Alex the other, but the only patch was on the back tire of a bike so rusted none of its parts moved.

So, the boys took off again, riding slowly down one road and up another, studying farmhouses, barns and outhouses of every kind. Finally, about noon, they stopped to eat. "It feels like we're wasting our time," said Coker.

"Duh. I guess. Let's think about who'd want to hide the bike and why. Maybe we can reason our way to it using our little gray cells." Alex and his mother watched *Hercule Poirot* on public television. He hoped it would sharpen his eyes in an investigation; she hoped it would turn his interest in detective work into an interest in English literature.

"Little what...? The answer's easy. They wanted to hide it because it would lead us to them and then we'd know who they were."

"So they're probably not going to put it at their house because that's too close, even though we'd never guess in a million years that they're there since we don't know where their house is."

"Yeah. Something like that. Right."

"Where would you hide a bike, Coker?"

Coker took a bite of his peanut butter sandwich and chewed for a minute. "I think I'd hide it in the woods where no one ever went."

"Until hunting season, then someone is almost everywhere."

"Yeah. But that's months off. And no one's looking for it anyway, except for us."

"We're not doing this right," Alex said, staring hard at his baloney. "We should be looking for where the bike was parked when the phantom wasn't riding it. Not the actual bike. Maybe we'd find out where he lived."

"Yeah. Maybe."

"So think. The guy was wearing a heavy overcoat. He's probably not going to ride far if he's got that thing on."

"Yeah."

"And he's not going to ride up and down a lot of steep hills. Especially in mud season."

"Yep."

"So, in the first place, wherever he lived, he lived not far from the museum, and probably in the direction we started out."

"But maybe not way down to Shrubsbury Center, because that's a hell of a steep hill."

"Right."

"So we should concentrate on the houses near the museum."

"Yeah, I'd say so."

"So let's go back." And they did, riding side by side, not really knowing what they'd do next.

"We must know someone who lives on that road," Alex shouted to Coker.

"Yeah, maybe more than one."

"How about Asa Parker?"

"Sure. How come we didn't think of him before?"

By the time the boys pedaled into Parker's drive, the sun was high in the sky and the day was warming. Lounging on the porch swing, drying new nail polish on her toes, was Zoe. Alex felt his face turn hot and red, but Coker seemed to have no problem at all. "Hey, Zoe," he called out and ambled over to where she sat.

"Hi yourself, Coker. What are you doing here?"

"We're trying to solve a mystery."

Godalmighty, thought Alex. I've got to stop this loose-mouthed idiot from saying too much. But it was hard to talk because Zoe's bare legs were beautiful and ended in the rose petal color of her toenail polish. He shifted from one foot to another.

"A mystery? Why would I know anything about that?" asked Zoe.

"You probably wouldn't," Alex answered before Coker could talk again. "And anyway we don't want to bore you with it, but was there a guy staying with your aunt and uncle who rode an old bicycle?"

"There was. I think he left. He was renting a room for a couple of months while he worked at Early's Auto in town."

"And he honest-to-God rode a crummy bike around?"

"Yeah. It was just borrowed from Uncle Asa. It's not like he took it into work or anything."

"Is the bike still here?" asked Alex.

"Probably. Behind the chicken house, I expect."

The boys walked over to discover a wreck of a bike leaning against the wall of the chicken house. It had a patch on the front wheel.

"Jeeze, Alex. What are we gonna do now?"

"We're gonna get Ms. M."

"Yeah, I think that's him," Asa Parker said, examining the photograph of the dead man. "Looks like he was in the water a long time so I'm not real sure. His name was Joel McPherson. He was working at Early's Auto as some kind of insurance consultant. Needed a place to stay off and on for a couple of months. God, I had no idea that he was the dead man. He left a note and took all his stuff. Thanked us, left a check for the days he'd promised. Seemed like a nice guy."

Tasha stood next to her son, the sheriff, and shook her head in astonishment. One thing after another. Was there a Joel McPherson? Was there a Max Fox? Why had Cornelia lied to her? She must have gotten to know Joel McPherson. Did she have something to do with the man's death after all? He must have been who he said he was. Nothing to do with Estey organs.

"Did he leave the bike here? How did you get it back after he was dead?"

"I don't know. It was just here again. I assumed he brought it back when he left the note."

"Thanks for the tip, boys, Mom," the sheriff said. "But try to stay far away from this business in the future. It's clear it has nothing to do with the museum. There's no reason for you to fool around with it. Someone murdered this guy. You don't want to get him excited."

"You're right, Stuart. Of course. This is your affair, not ours. We won't play detective anymore."

Ms. M and Alex went to their meeting place in the graveyard later in the afternoon, but they lied to Coker and Lori about where they'd gone. Ms. M was taking a nap. Her age you know. Every once in a while it caught up with her. Alex had one more homework assignment, a last hurrah from his seventh grade teacher and an opening salvo from his eighth. They lied to Coker because Alex thought he was beginning to be liability (movie language). They lied to Lori because as soon as she left they planned on using her computer. Their lies were earnest. No one would have doubted them for a moment.

"Has your son checked on Joel McPherson yet, Ms. M?"

The Organist Who Wore Gloves

"He's probably not going to tell me when he does. It's a shame, but our families don't believe in our partnership, Alex. He won't say a word about it to me."

"Huh! He's lucky some of us have imagination. I've been thinking we should look at the note the guy left with Mr. Parker, and see if the handwriting is the same on it as on the globe."

Ms. M chuckled. "That's a great idea, Alex, but I'm afraid Mr. Parker said he threw it away. It had been a a little while after all. We'll just have to work quietly on our own set of clues. As soon as Lori's left and no one's around, we'll go to the office and do some investigating."

"What will you do about Mrs. Early?" Alex asked, and took a big bite out of a newly baked ginger cookie.

"I'll have to confront her again. I don't want to but she's left me with no choice. I'll go see her after dinner."

"I have a question about all that. Don't you think Mrs. Early's husband would have noticed if she was bringing more money home than his brother should have been paying her?"

"Yes. I do. You're a perceptive guy, Alex. It's

possible he just took advantage of it. He's smart. He's a banker—he knows money. He's been a part-time reporter for the newspaper for years now and, granted the local paper is no *New York Times*, he's written lots of financial stories."

"That would make him worse than she is."

"I'd say so. It would also make him a suspect if the dead man were Cornelia's blackmailer. Are you enjoying the cookies?"

"Do you think she knows he knows? I think ginger snaps are my favorite now."

"No. I think she'd prefer to think he doesn't. Cornelia's like that, you know. What she wants to be true becomes it. I remember a cocktail party she and Colin gave last year. He's a terrible bartender, but she's always found him masterful. We all suffered. Anyway, I'm not certain of anything. I'm speculating. You do know that, don't you?"

"Yep. If it's like last time, we know all sorts of things we probably don't know."

Ms. M smiled ruefully. "So we probably have three suspects: Cornelia and Colin Early and the other guy who might be the blackmailer. And maybe Bob Early or his wife."

"What would their motives be, Ms. M?"

"I'm not sure."

"Maybe Bob Early would want to get even with Cornelia Early and so he'd kill the guy and make it look like she did it."

"He certainly hasn't done that. Make her look guilty of murder. Not yet, anyway."

"Yeah. How about this one? Bob Early knows she's a crook, and maybe he doesn't want anyone else to know because she's his sister-in-law and he doesn't want to look stupid."

"Sounds terribly overwrought, Alex. I don't know."

They watched Lori drive away, and taking care to look like they were going somewhere they weren't, they walked, one at a time, back to the Timothy Evensong House.

"She was watching us, you know. First me. Then you," Alex said, opening a window and turning on the computer.

"Who, Alex?"

"Serendipity Hamilton, your odd, odd neighbor."

"I guess she doesn't have anything else to do with her day."

"I hope that's it," he said.

They settled in and Alex began the search for Joel McPherson. "Sounds like a baseball player, doesn't he?"

"The dead man certainly didn't look like one."

"I don't find anyone he might be when I google the name, although there is a kid by that name who pitched for his high school. Why don't I look at Early's Auto before we get really serious?"

"Go for it."

Early's Auto was almost entirely ads for cars, used and new. Cornelia's e-mail was given on the list of staff, but there was nothing else about her. Bob Early was mentioned several times as the owner. There was nothing about insurance and certainly nothing about anyone named Joel.

"I'm going to try coming at it from a completely different direction. Let's look at pump organs and stuff and see if we find his name."

But there was no Joel, not anywhere, who had to do with music or with cars.

XIV

That evening, Tasha looked for Cornelia, but no one was home. The next day, people at the auto company told her Mrs. Early had taken a few days off; they didn't know where she'd gone. Yes, they remembered Joel. Nice guy. Back at the house at lunchtime, Colin Early told her his wife needed a rest and had gone to the coast to watch waves and sea birds. He didn't know exactly where she was. And no, he had no time to talk just now. He'd been overwhelmed by work assignments. He didn't know anything about the dead gentleman; he didn't know anything about Cornelia's acquaintance with him, but she met many people in the course of her job that he didn't know. He had phone calls to make. He'd have Cornelia call Tasha as soon as she returned home.

"I feel so frustrated, Alex," she said, reporting to

him back at the museum where he was helping dig up a spot for the school garden. "What do you think we should do next?"

"Sounds like we have to wait," Alex said, resting for a moment with his chin on the handle of his shovel.

"I'm going to spend some time in the museum this afternoon as soon as everyone's gone for the day. I want to try to remember what my ex-husband said about his life in this town and his experiences hanging out around the museum."

"I thought you probably already did that."

"Not sitting in the museum. Not really concentrating. No. I haven't wanted to. It was one of my least favorite times."

"Like school is mine."

"Sort of," she smiled fondly at him. Every time she nearly shared her past troubles with him, he brought her up short and she realized again that he was a kid. And not even her kid.

So, just as she had when she was at the end of her patience in the case of the body in the butter churn, she went into the museum to think, but not in the kitchen this time. In the music room. In fact, she sat at the keyboard of the Estey while she tried to remember what she knew of Max in this space.

Max had spent part of his growing up at the Evensong House across the road, only then the house had belonged to one of the many Parkers in the village. Max's family was poor and so he was sent to board and apprentice with Henry Parker. They hoped he might learn some of Henry's carpentry skills and, at the same time, earn enough to help feed his family. Since Max was an enterprising sort of person and curious about everything, Parker also put him in charge of the museum. For a little cash, the Parkers had been its groundkeepers ever since they'd moved in across the road decades earlier. Max spent hours exploring and cleaning the museum and, as he learned more, guiding occasional visitors through it.

Probably nothing impressed Max like the musical instruments in the place: the harmonium, the many melodeons, the parlor organ. He and his friends—who were his friends, she tried to remember—a boy named Bob, a girl called Sara—they had tried to make a band of the instruments and, since it was still the mid-1950s, practiced a form of jazz, not rock. But because they were smart and eclectic, they mixed it up with classical works and country tunes. Because there were adults around and they wanted to keep them out, they also played some pious hymn tunes.

"We really grooved. Got some pots and pans for percussion; one of the boys brought his dad's fiddle. The place had wonderful acoustics, at least for the sound we wanted to make."

She remembered that what he really wanted was the sound of Fats Waller on the pipe organ playing "Sugar." "He played it on an honest-to-God Estey organ! They made it for him. Can you imagine?" Max crowed.

She'd laughed. She remembered she'd laughed. It was so like Max. For a moment she forgot what happened later and remembered him fondly. She listened and heard the thumping of feet, the rattle of pots, the wheezing of many organs, the occasional squeal of a fiddle gone crazy. That was what they did when you played them with a stiff and insensitive bow. They squealed.

Tasha Mulholland listened and she heard it all, and thought again how sad it was that not one of the melodeons and organs was played today. They'd been created to be played in churches and parlors. People had worshipped with them, courted to their melodies, and entertained themselves for hours at home and in church halls. Now, they were preserved in silence even though they'd been created to sing. The museum was their mausoleum. Max and his gang had probably been the last people to play many of them.

Max had described a few teen affairs during his Old Shrubsbury School days. None of them went very far. The Parkers were a conservative bunch, even by the codes of that day. Max thought he was in love with one of the girls, was it Sara or…. Why did she have so much trouble with the other one? Sara and…. Or maybe Sera. Maybe it was Serendipity who played with them. She lived a few hundred feet down the road. But she would have been much younger, just a little kid.

All the same she would talk to Sera. But the other name…. why had she lost it? She looked up just in time to see someone passing through the room, a ghostly person, a woman who smiled continually. Most ghosts didn't. It wasn't a prized form of existence.

Was that the woman who used to play with Max's band?

The Organist Who Wore Gloves

He called her Connie. Was her real name Cornelia?

She stirred and played a few odd notes on the organ. She wasn't going to risk the health of a near ancient musical instrument—perhaps, if it had been a cello….

Tasha got up from the organ and paced around the room. What could the phantom organ player have been doing here? If anything material, a note or a formula, whatever, had been hidden in a musical instrument, surely someone would have found it long ago. All of these musical heirlooms had been studied by people who knew what they were looking at and, in the case of the phantom, playing. Was that what she was missing? The playing of it? Did the secret, if there was one, arise from the playing of the organ?

She went back to press a few notes, the opening of the "Toccata and Fugue," Fats Waller's "Sugar"—that was all she knew that Max Fox, the phantom in the overcoat, had played. Some really terrible combination of the two. There might be something in the combination of notes, in the keys…. The key. "Open Door." The solution seemed so close, and yet so far. But Max, her husband, had collected musical puzzles. Almost certainly, this was one. She just had to figure it out.

XV

Why was it that night that Tasha woke to the sound of an organ playing "Sugar?" She threw on a coat and shoes and headed over to the museum, feeling anxious, and not a little angry. Wasn't he dead—the phantom organist? Who was it then? Why was he back? She crept into the museum through the kitchen door this time, but even before she'd opened it the music stopped. When she went into the music room no one was there, and she didn't hear anyone leave. The room looked undisturbed, although the bench was at the same slight angle. She searched the place with her flashlight, and then climbed the stairs as quietly as she could—but there really was no way to climb them in complete silence. They groaned no matter how carefully she made her way up. She went directly to Evensong's room to scan the slate globe. It

The Organist Who Wore Gloves

was part of a poem by Elizabeth Barrett Browning. She wasn't sure the handwriting was the same as the Whitman poem, but on a rough curved surface like the globe it could have been.

He cut it short, did the great god Pan,

(How tall it stood in the river!)

Then drew the pith, like the heart of a man,

Steadily from the outside ring,

And notched the poor dry empty thing

In holes, as he sate by the river.

"This is the way," laughed the great god Pan,

(Laughed while he sat by the river,)

"The only way, since gods began

To make sweet music, they could succeed."

Then, dropping his mouth to a hole in the reed,

He blew in power by the river.

Elaine Magalis

Sweet, sweet, sweet, O Pan!

Piercing sweet by the river!

Blinding sweet, O great god Pan!

The sun on the hill forgot to die,

And the lilies revived, and the dragon-fly

Came back to dream on the river.

Yet half a beast is the great god Pan,

To laugh as he sits by the river,

Making a poet out of a man:

The true gods sigh for the cost and pain,—

For the reed which grows nevermore again

As a reed with the reeds in the river.

"Reeds. An organ might depend on the deaths of many reeds, many more than a flute," murmured Tasha. A rather depressing view of the world. Not like what she thought she knew of Max Fox.

The Organist Who Wore Gloves

She didn't sleep the rest of that night. She waited impatiently for Alex to appear in the morning, worrying the whole night that she was exposing a child to adventures he was too young to deal with. Remembering that his teacher once called her a bad influence.

"Do you think he was a ghost?" Alex asked.

"No, I don't. I'm quite sure he wasn't." She said it with conviction, but she kept remembering that he'd disappeared without a sound. No footsteps, no doors opening or closing, no bicycle, no car.

"But then, he's not dead. And if he's not dead, who is?"

Tasha Mulholland smiled at him helplessly. "I have no idea," she said.

XVI

She called Serendipity Hamilton and invited herself to a brunch of coffee and croissants. The two women sat on the terrace in the bright morning, and exchanged pleasantries for five minutes until neither one of them could bear it any longer. "So, Tasha, why did you invite yourself to my table? Why are you here?"

"This may seem strange to you, Sera, but I wondered if you could try to remember my late husband, Maxwell. I know you were only a child when he was a teenager growing up at the Parker house...."

"I was five years old then. Awfully young. I do, however, have a nearly record book long-term memory."

"So you do have memories of that time?"

"Yes. I was quite taken with your Maxwell, you know."

"Hmmmm, yes. Not long after, I was too," Tasha said ruefully.

"I never understood how and why you let him go. It was just a little midlife crisis. Not a problem. He would have recovered."

"I suppose you're right," she responded, and didn't mean a word of it. "What do you remember about him, Sera?"

"He was so smart. He knew everything."

"About...."

"We went on hikes up Prospect Hill. I remember at the top he taught us to yodel. I can still do it." She drew herself up, her purple bosom swelling. She breathed in and opened her mouth. "Lady o de lady o de leh hee hoo." Her highs and her lows were both remarkable. So she did it again. "Lady o de lady o de leh heeee hoooooooo."

"Very impressive. Very impressive indeed. We had the same teacher." And Tasha yodeled back, just as loudly, just as long. Alex, wandering around looking for clues around the doors and windows of the museum, was incredulous. What was she doing now—his old lady partner? Maybe he should have gone with her.

Tasha and Serendipity were laughing together, Sera spewing a mouthful of coffee across the table.

"He loved music, didn't he?" asked Tasha.

"He turned us into a band. He had a record of some big black man playing an organ."

"Fats Waller playing 'Sugar'?"

"Yes. I guess that's who it was. He played 'Sugar' for us, and we all played with him—the other organs, buckets, even the stairs in the building became instruments. The noise was incredible."

"Didn't Old Man Parker hear you? And what about your mother?"

"No, I think he was already deaf. And my mother was busy with other matters."

"Do you remember if Max had a girlfriend?"

"You know, I don't. I mean that was a few years before you, wasn't it?"

The Organist Who Wore Gloves

"Was there someone named Connie?"

"You mean Cornelia."

"Cornelia Early?"

"Yes. Her. I was so jealous of her.... She hung on him all the time."

"But you were just a kid...."

"Yes. That was the problem. I couldn't wait to grow up."

"Do you remember Max being very, very serious? Pledging everyone to secrecy about something? Anything like that."

"What an odd question, Tasha. Did he ever tell you about something like that?"

"I think he might have. But I didn't take it seriously. I don't remember, I'm afraid."

"This is all about the dead man, isn't it? He plays the organ in the museum at night and the next thing you know you're thinking about Max."

"How do you know about the organ?"

"I have ears, my dear Tasha. I have ears. And I don't

sleep very well at the best of times. Besides, I know that music. 'Sugar.' And Bach's whatever it was…."

"Did you ever try to find out why he was there? Did you try to catch him playing and ask him who he was and why he was there in freezing temperatures?"

"No. I don't exhibit myself after midnight. I need full makeup to go out into the world. I never knew when he would show up."

"Who did you think it was?"

"Oh, I thought it was Maxwell. Your husband. Who else?"

Tasha caught her breath. "He's dead, Sera. He's been dead for years."

"No. And he wasn't that poor bastard in the pond either."

"Why do you think Max is still alive?"

"I don't know. I never believed he died. Why did you?"

"You never saw him again? I mean, after he left here. After he left me and Stuart and went to Brattleboro?"

"No. I never did. My mother sent me away to school. But I always knew somehow that he was alive."

"He wasn't, Sera. He's dead and he's been dead for years."

Serendipity shrugged her shoulders and refilled their coffee cups.

XVII

Alex studied the grass in front of the museum, looking for something that would prove the phantom had been there the night before. There was no sign of a bicycle. He knew Ms. M had already searched the music room and Evensong's study, but he looked again. Except for the poem, there was nothing new or changed anywhere. He sat down on the porch outside the kitchen and stared across the grass to the horizon. It seemed to him that they had to find Cornelia Early. Especially if Ms. M was right and she'd played in the museum with the phantom's father those many years ago. He wished there was another cigarette butt. Another Camel. But he didn't find one. There was no new evidence anywhere.

"I've just made an appointment with Colin Early, Alex."

The Organist Who Wore Gloves

"For when? Can I come too?"

"I don't think you should. You're not good at small talk, at least not yet. No one is going to say anything revealing in front of you, sweetie. You can spy on us. I give you leave to do that. But be careful. Colin could be dangerous. Although I admit, it's hard for me to imagine him hurting a soul."

After lunch Alex started collecting games for the children who were coming in a few days to a special 4-H Day. He set out the stilts, the game of Graces, the hoops and the nine-pins, but when he saw Ms. M starting off in her yellow truck, he leapt onto his bike and followed her. She'd given him permission to spy, and he would.

By the time he got to the Early home, she'd been there for ten minutes. He found her through a peephole in the fence, sitting at the side of the pool with Colin Early, his brother Bob, and Adele, Bob's wife. The pool was still a blue waterless hole; the weather wasn't warm enough yet to fill it.

"I had no idea Cornelia was that much in need of a vacation. She's not really sick, is she?"

"I hadn't any idea she was so exhausted either. And

wound tight…! I guess we're both getting older. Did I get your drink right? I love bartending. You should come over more often."

"I've never drunk a better Harvey Wallbanger!"

Harvey what? thought Alex. What kind of name is that for a drink? Adults were so strange, especially the old ones.

"I don't think it has anything to do with age, Colin," said Adele Early. "She's been working too hard. I hope you had her checked out with the doctor before you sent her off on this so-called vacation."

"Just a few days ago. She checked out fine," said Colin and looked at her, smiling, as if he were comforting a small child.

"I should hope so," she responded. Alex was surprised. It seemed to him that Adele Early and her brother-in-law didn't like each other. He'd ask Ms. M about it later.

"How's business, Bob?" Tasha asked. "I've been so happy with my yellow truck. I'll be forever grateful to you for finding it for me."

The Organist Who Wore Gloves

"Hey, you're one of my favorite customers."

"Even though I only check in with you every ten or so years?"

"Even though…."

"And business is good?"

"Never better."

"Is it true that the body we discovered in the pond at the museum was Joel McPherson and that he worked with you at the dealership?" she asked abruptly.

"Yes. I never identified the body, but it must have been if Parker says so. Nice guy. Kept to himself."

"What did he do for you? I didn't know you had people working there who were from away."

"We don't advertise it," he said smiling. "It's a home-grown business and everyone is supposed to be a local. Joel was consulting with us. He was an expert on a defect in some of our cars and trucks. We had to call back a large number and he was helping us here and in St. Johnsbury with the recall."

"So none of you ever got to know him well?"

"No. I think the Parkers knew him better than anybody. It's hard to understand why anyone would want to kill him."

"It is, isn't it?"

"Don't tell me you and that kid are still doing detective work?"

"Just a little. Don't tell Stuart."

"Wouldn't dream of it. But be careful, Tasha. There's apparently a murderer running around. We wouldn't want anything to happen to either one of you."

"We'll be careful, Bob," she said. "I'm grateful for your concern."

She dipped a cheese cracker in a dip on the table and nibbled at it. "My goodness, Colin, this dip is delicious. You must tell me how you made it."

"Store bought. I've got no talent for such things. Nor does Cornelia. She's more into things musical and numerical."

"Which brings up one of the reasons I wanted to talk to your wife, but you fellows probably remember just as well. Didn't you all hang out with Max at the museum when you were teenagers?"

"Oh, yes. Max was one of our best influences. We had a lot of fun at the museum. He got us to help him with his job there. We formed an odd lot musical group and made a huge racket."

"Was Sera Hamilton one of the gang, even though she was much younger?"

"Yeah. Much younger. And scary as hell!"

"Scary. How odd? What did she do?"

"Swung from trees, tap danced down the stairs, tried to get us to play ball with the globe, you know the chalkboard one? She took all the dolls from their exhibits to give them baths. And I swear she tried to do away with Connie—that's what it looked like to us. She wanted your future husband all to herself."

"How?"

"Pushed her down the stairs several times. And tried to run her over with her bike."

"Oh, dear. That does sound like Sera. Were you all part of Max's band?"

"Oh, yes. We played everything in the museum that

would make any sound at all."

"And the music—Bach's 'Toccata and Fugue'"?

"I guess that's what it was. Mostly I remember this Fats Waller number. Max would play it on the old Estey."

Alex had always thought Bob Early was a nice man, and he still did, but he didn't know about Colin who was stirring his rum and whatever and staring out at his pool. He looked forlorn. Was he missing his wife that much? Or was something else going on?

"Max had a lot of influence on all of you, I guess."

"With all respect to your past husband, Tasha, I think it was all for the bad," said Adele. "They're entirely too happy go lucky. I've been trying ever since I came here to get this important businessman to pay attention to his books. If it wasn't for Cornelia, Early's Auto would have gone down the tubes a long time ago."

"We were happy kids," Bob said, ignoring his wife. "Colin and I had good parenting, and we were pretty solid citizens, even then. But Max taught us how to have fun."

"Tell me something, Tasha," said Colin Early. "I've

never known you to talk much about your ex. Is this just sentimental old age, or something else?"

"I'll be honest with you, Colin. Someone has been playing Max's favorite music on the Estey in the museum. It's eerie and it's made me both nervous and nostalgic."

"You're kidding. That's weird, isn't it?"

"Are you sure you're not having hallucinations? Maybe Cornelia's isn't the only mind that's feeling its age," said Adele.

"No. I've had collaboration from young people with good ears. Anyway, I've been sharing my concerns about it with Cornelia. I really wish she were around to talk with me about it."

"Did she have any guesses about who it might be?"

"No. At least, she wouldn't say."

"She didn't think it was a ghost, did she?" Bob interrupted with a laugh.

"Cornelia's never seemed to me to be one to believe in ghosts," Tasha said. "She's pretty level-headed. Which is why I need her. My imagination just takes flight, you know?"

"You don't actually think the organ player might be your husband?" he said.

"Oh no. Of course not. Not really. But ever since we found that body in the pond...."

"Stuart can't find out anything about Joel McPherson?"

"Not yet anyway. But I'm sure he had to do with the night activities at the museum. And now that the organ music has started again...."

"I can't imagine why you think Cornelia could be of any help."

"She has a very important relationship to the museum. I know for a fact that Cornelia knows quite a lot. I think she may even know who he was and who killed him. At the very least she knows more than anyone else about what's going on."

"Cornelia has always talked too much," Adele said. Alex watched Bob Early give her a nasty look.

"Excuse me. I'm going to go in and see if I can chase down some more ice," Bob said, rising suddenly.

"I know she's at the museum a lot," Colin said. "I know she has some fond memories, just as I do. But there's nothing else, Tasha. My wife has no secrets from you, from me, from anyone."

"Oh, now Colin. Everyone has some secrets, even and maybe especially Cornelia," said Adele.

"Just please let me know when she comes back," Tasha interrupted. "She and I were having an important conversation we really need to finish."

"I've brought some more rum if anyone wants to liven up their drink," Bob said, coming back out onto the terrace.

"I really couldn't," said Tasha. "And shouldn't. But thank you, Bob. It's so lovely back here," she added and leaned back in her chair.

"Yeah, isn't it wonderful," Colin responded. "Cornelia loves sitting out here, especially at this time of day."

Having determined that none of them were going to tell her more, Tasha finished her Harvey Wallbanger and walked back to her truck, deep in thought, leaving the brothers and Adele sitting by the pool. Alex heard her get into her yellow truck and start it. Everyone was quiet—and dour, thought Alex. It was one of his favorite new words.

"What do you think, Bob?" asked Colin.

"You know what I think," Bob replied. "I hope I've taken care of the problem."

Alex crept away, grabbed his bike and headed out. He didn't know what to make of any of it. The men seemed affable. Adele Early seemed angry, but maybe she was always that way. The stories seemed like old ones, with almost nothing to do with the present. None of the Earlys seemed to have any idea Cornelia Early might be an embezzler.

XVIII

Alex rode away, trying to think. He was in no hurry to get to the museum or to head home. Why hadn't Ms. M really confronted those guys? They had to know sooner or later that Mrs. Early was a crook if they didn't know already. Ms. M might as well be the one to tell them. Someone would soon. She used to be much gutsier, his Ms. M. Whatever was wrong with her?

Maybe he should be more helpful. Maybe he should talk to the Sheriff and tell him about Cornelia, even though the guy didn't want to talk to him. The solution to the murder was within reach, he thought, if only they would confront the guilty.

That's when he heard something, somewhere. A crash. Like a car had run off the road, knocking into trees as it went. Probably his imagination, but he sped up because he was scared. He didn't know why. A few minutes later he got to Rabbit Hill. It was muddier than usual. There had been rain the night before. There were deep tracks all over, running left and running right. Like teenagers having a good time. Not just teenagers. He recognized one set of tracks, the yellow truck's tracks. He knew that Ms. M was no kid doing kooky things in her yellow truck. The tracks ran left and right, twisting and turning and then ending just where the road took a sharp turn. He went down the hill fast, staying on the right, to the side, avoiding all the mud, then taking the corner and flying to the edge of the road to ditch the bike and run. The truck at the bottom of the hill looked like a big yellow bird that some numbskull hunter had shot, and left for dead because it had broken its back and lay in the trees in its death throes, twitching helplessly.

He ran to it. The cab was upside down; one wheel was still spinning. He couldn't see inside. Was she there? Was she okay? He tried to open a door on the driver's side then ran to the other door, which was open and hanging by a hinge. No Ms. M there. He'd kill whoever hurt her.

He felt a sob catch in his throat as he searched the brush for her. He stumbled back onto the road, through something that looked very like poison ivy. She was sitting next to the gully, leaning against a rock, as if she were waiting for a ride. "Alex. Am I ever glad to see you. Would you phone 911, and get my son over here? I think I've been sabotaged."

He went straight to her, put both arms around her, and sobbed. "Hey Alex, I'm okay. Poor guy. It's all right, sweetie."

Alex took the Kleenex she offered him, blew hard, and made the telephone call. He affected a dry, straightforward report. "There's a truck off the road on Rabbit Hill. It looks like it turned over a couple of times—totaled I think—and there's a lady here hurt. Could you send someone 'round?"

"I'll send them right out. Who are you, son?"

"I'm Alex Churchill."

"Were you in the accident, Alex?"

"No, ma'am. Just came on it."

"How's the lady doing?"

"She's very pale and her head is bleeding. I think she may have broke her arm too."

"Is she conscious?"

"Yeah, but she looks as if she might faint on me. Get somebody here quick, would you?"

"I will, Alex." He hung up before the woman could ask him more questions.

"You wanna lie down, Ms. M?"

"I'd rather not. Surely, it's not totaled. Do you really think it's that bad?"

"What happened?"

"I think someone fooled with my brakes. They're not happy about all the questions I've been asking, I guess. Would you promise me you'll be very, very careful? Don't ask anyone anything until we've had a chance to talk again. In fact, don't ask anyone anything at all. And for the sake of all that's holy, don't say anything to anybody about my suspicions. Just say you figure I was going too fast and missed the turn." She stopped talking, breathless, as if she'd run down and hit bottom all over again.

"Yes, ma'am. Here, you lean up against me." He slipped down next to her and draped one arm loosely around her shoulders. "You stop talking now. I won't do anything to make things worse. I promise."

For Alex, the rest of the day was awful. As soon as the ambulance and the police car came, he was ignored. Ms. M was gently lifted onto a stretcher (you can bet she hated that!), and taken to Newport Hospital. The police studied the truck but no one asked Alex anything for what seemed like forever until finally, Stuart came over to him.

"Are the two of you still trying to be detectives?"

"No sir. Ms. M had just gone in search of Mrs. Early because she hadn't come to work. I went for a bike ride and accidentally found her. Then I called 911. She's going to be okay, isn't she?"

"She'll be fine. You go back to the museum. I gather your workday isn't over."

"You know your mother drives a little fast?"

"You're right, Alex. She sure does. You don't forget and go and do likewise. Hear?"

But Alex knew the accident didn't have to do with Ms. Mulholland's driving, however awful it was. The truck had been tampered with. He hoped the sheriff would figure it out since Ms. M wouldn't let him say anything about it. Probably it was Bob. That's what he did when he left the terrace for a few minutes, when Alex assumed he was just going to take a leak or break up some ice. When he came back he claimed that he had "taken care" of something. What? Alex asked himself. But he was pretty sure he knew what.

XIX

Tasha was out of the hospital by the next day and looking as lively as ever, even though she wore a sling and she'd been told to rest. Alex's mother had taken stock of how upset he was. Clearly, Ms. M remained a central figure in her son's life. She'd always liked her. Her own parents were no longer alive and grandparents were important. What could she do? She'd let him visit the old woman whenever he asked. He idolized her. And who else would ever be able to answer all the questions he asked every day?

So Alex brought a tuna casserole from his mother, and pages of printouts from his computer. He'd been googling Estey organs, organ music, and Brattleboro. He left it all with her while he took Gusty for a walk. When he came back, she was in a state of high excitement.

"This is wonderful, Alex. You've done superb work. I'm so grateful. Max loved to fool with mathematical formulas and music, Bach of course, but really any music."

"So you think Max had a secret that someone could figure out from the music?"

"Yes. And I'll bet we could figure it out. It won't be that hard. But it's just as exciting that you found Noah Patrovsky, the old man in Brattleboro. I'll write to him right away."

"Does it hurt where your arm broke?"

"A little. It's just a tiny break." The doorbell rang. "That's Stuart. He wants to talk about the accident. If you stay, you have to be quiet. Okay? Let me do the talking."

Alex promised. But he wouldn't have had to because Sheriff Stuart Mulholland assumed that since he was a kid he wouldn't have anything to say anyway.

"Okay, Mom," said Stuart. "I want to know. Are you aware that your brake lines might have been cut by someone and that your so-called accident might not be an accident at all?"

The Organist Who Wore Gloves

"Yes, Stuart."

"And do you have any idea of who that someone might be?"

"No. Not so I'd say."

"What does that mean? I'm not asking for proof positive of anything. Do you have any suspicions? Can you guess why?"

"Well, yes then I can guess. But I'm not going to, Stuart. I don't know, and I don't want to accuse anybody unjustly."

"Oh, for God's sake, Mom. I'm not going to go around arresting anyone without proof. You know that."

"Stuart, I could ruin some lives if I talk before I know more than I do now. You'll just have to be patient with me. Now, if you want to ask me what I was doing before I went off Rabbit Hill into a ditch, I'll tell you."

"You were coming back to the museum after a visit with Colin Early. Bob and Adele were there also. You were there because Cornelia hadn't come to the museum for a few days and you wanted to make sure she was okay."

"Exactly."

"Is she?"

"You mean is she okay? Yes, I guess. She was all tired out and went somewhere to rest. Her husband won't say exactly where."

"So it wasn't a very useful meeting. You didn't find out anything."

"I found out that the most important people in her life were certain she was fine. So I felt considerably relieved and left in a better mood than when I came."

"That's good, isn't it? You didn't accuse them of anything awful, did you? Something that would make them want to kill you?"

"I didn't accuse them of anything, Stuart. I've known the Early boys forever. We had a drink together and everyone was happy. Would you like some tuna casserole for lunch?"

Alex sighed. The man hadn't acknowledged his existence. He'd even gone to see him the evening before and shared the Camel butts with him along with photos of where he'd found them, the dates and the condition of the butts. Evidence! But nothing had changed. He might as well have been a fly buzzing in the kitchen, or a flea on Winky the cat. Another dull brown bird in a world full of sparrows. Nobody.

XX

Tasha Mulholland sat by the window, looking out at the museum and studying the printouts Alex had brought her, a cup of coffee called Meditation in front of her. She remembered how much music had meant to her husband. It was a passion they had shared. If there was a clue in what the phantom organist was playing, it should be something she could uncover. She remembered that Max also loved numbers:

He'd quoted Leibniz, "Music is the pleasure the human mind experiences from counting without being aware that it is counting."

Somewhere, in those two very different pieces of music—Bach's "Toccata and Fugue" and Fats Waller's "Sugar"—somewhere there was the answer to a puzzle.

Had Max put it there simply to make people a little crazy? Maybe. That wasn't unlike him. But it was just as likely that whatever the answer was it was at the heart of the whole mystery.

It was also clear that whatever it was, it began in that summer before the museum was really a museum, when Max was a kid, when a bunch of kids, all grown now, played music in the museum.

What was almost as exciting was that her twelve-going-on-thirteen-year-old partner had started a friendship with another elderly person, Noah Patrovsky, a man she remembered with pleasure—Max's friend and someone present at the Estey Organ Factory when Max fell from the catwalk and died. Alex had actually e-mailed the man and described the organ-playing phantom, the murder, the trip to Brattleboro, all of it. He'd introduced her without her knowledge, and invited the gentleman to visit Shrubsbury. "Ms. M isn't able to travel now because she got hurt by someone who thought she knew too much."

Noah Patrovsky had written back. Because he was 101, he said, his friends wouldn't let him drive the miles to Shrubsbury, but he'd be more than happy to exchange e-mail with Alex and Ms. Mulholland, and they were welcome to visit him at any time.

Dear Noah, she replied. It's so wonderful to be in touch with you again. I remember visiting you with Max years ago. You played the organ for us, I think the 'Toccata and Fugue.' You were extraordinary.

Alex seems to have told you most of what's been going on here. You can imagine that I've been anxious, worrying that Max Fox, the dead man, was Max's son. Now that someone's been playing the organ in the museum again, I'm just confused. We need to figure out what Max shared with his circle of young people those many years ago, and what's happened to it since it may have something to do with the death of his son.

I'd love to visit you. I broke my arm when my truck lost its brakes on a hill. (We suspect they were cut deliberately!) The break isn't bad and otherwise I'm just a little shaken. However, my truck has been totaled. I'm going to try to get another vehicle as soon as possible. In the meantime, anything you can tell me about Max and music on his last and fatal trip to Brattleboro would be of help.

Best regards, Tasha Mulholland

The Organist Who Wore Gloves

Alex bicycled her words to his house and his computer and got an answer in minutes, as if the man had been sitting waiting for something exciting to happen.

Dear Tasha, he wrote, I remember you too, and our evening together. I'm so sorry that yours and Max's relationship didn't last, but as I've been married and divorced four times, I can't say I'm surprised.

The reason Max came to Brattleboro, as I understood it, was to find the Estey organ that had been in your museum, the organ he'd played as a youngster. It was in our shop to be refurbished and refreshed. It was returned to your museum a short time later. There was something about that instrument he loved, but I can't tell you what. He didn't tell me.

I can assure you there was nothing suspicious about Max's death. The catwalk had been damaged, but as it was in part of the factory that had already been closed down no one thought to issue a warning, or to repair it. Max drifted in there when the conversations about the future of the factory became too cantankerous. We were losing money fast, and there was no chance that the business could be revived, but some among us just didn't want to quit so the quarrels went on and on. Max grew bored and wandered off.

I found out that Belinda was pregnant after Max's death. I don't think Max knew. She hadn't told anyone yet. I can't tell you why Gerald Must remembers the situation differently. He's become more and more irascible with old age. I, too, heard that Belinda died a short time ago, and you may be right to suspect that one of the men haunting your museum in the dead of the night is Max's son. I knew the young man, and the photograph doesn't quite look like him. Perhaps the condition of the body....

Max Fox is a nice young man; he loves music just the way his father did and seems to have the same mischievous nature. It's probably genetic. I, however, always thought Belinda was rather sour.

I hope I've been of some help. I don't know that I can tell you anything more. I look forward to your visit. The sooner the better since I'm quite ancient and may not be around much longer.

Faithfully yours, Noah Patrovsky

So Belinda was "rather sour," Tasha noted when she read his letter, embarrassed that she was happy to hear it.

The Organist Who Wore Gloves

When Alex returned after a long afternoon cleaning the Education Center, the two sleuths shared the rest of the ginger cookies, and thought about the Estey organ and what secret the music played on it might harbor.

Said Tasha, "Both are in the same key, and both are in 4/4 time. However, 'Sugar,' is allegro, or fast, and the beginning of the 'Toccata and Fugue' is adagio, slow; they're utterly different in mood.

"It could be that the question is: Is there also something different about the music played on this instrument? In fact, different in the same way for both pieces? After all, this is a reed organ and not a pipe. Both organ pieces are usually played on a pipe. How will the reed organ change both pieces? It will make much less volume and less tonal range..... 'Sugar,' doesn't need much tonal range. Or volume. But the 'Toccata and Fugue' does."

"Ms M, I don't get it. Where's the puzzle? Are you sure this is the way to go?"

"I am. You just wait. Sooner or later, we'll get it."

"I don't even know what a toccata is."

"It's a fast piece of music, Alex. Light and fast. The word comes from the Italian word 'to touch.'"

"To touch and sugar. Those are the words for the music that has the secret."

"Yes. Very soon we'll have figured it out."

"And then what?"

"We'll know what the point of all of this was."

"Oh boy. I hope it's gonna be worth it."

XXI

There were days when Alex's mother left for work before five in the morning. Usually, hearing her in the kitchen, Alex woke up, turned over, and went back to sleep. On this day, though, he started thinking, which seemed to him to be a sign that he should get up and do something significant, so he dressed, grabbed a granola bar, and took off on his bicycle.

It was still dark; dawn was just beginning to whiten the sky when he rolled up to the museum. He wouldn't have stopped—not this early—but he saw a small flickering light in the music room. He stopped, blinked, let his bike fall to the ground and headed for the only window where the shade fell just lopsided enough to see inside. There she was, no surprise somehow, Cornelia Early with a flashlight, bent over the organ bench, looking for something. She looked eerie in the glow of her light, a pale green face framed by a black hood. She seemed to know the organ well. When she couldn't find what she wanted in the bench, she removed the back panel of the instrument and peered inside. But she couldn't find it there either. She reattached it and sat on the bench, her back to the instrument, her body hunched over in despair. Then, suddenly, she looked around as if she'd heard something but didn't know where the sound was coming from. Alex knew it wasn't him: he hadn't moved, not even a little. She moved quickly out of his view. He heard her walking, almost scampering, to the kitchen door and he threw himself down on the ground against the museum wall, hoping she wouldn't see him.

Cornelia Early didn't see Alex, but she did see his bicycle. He saw her stop and stare, then turn quickly towards the road and run, not walk, to the black car parked there—her car. He would have tried to follow, but she pulled out too fast and sped off. Was she going home? There was no way of knowing. Not really. But, he thought, it might be a good idea to go there and stake her out.

It was still too early to wake up Ms. M and besides,

he thought, she should rest. He didn't have a key to the museum but he thought it was unlikely he would find something Mrs. Early hadn't. It wasn't until he was well on his way to her house that he thought he should have waited to see if there was anyone else in the museum. Maybe the organist. Alive or dead.

At the Early house, Colin Early was seated at the breakfast table, drinking coffee, looking at what seemed to be the financial pages of the newspaper. There was no evidence that his wife was there. One coffee cup. One piece of toast. One newspaper. Alex crept around to the garage and looked in the window. One car. Colin Early's green Buick Park Avenue. Cornelia's black Impala was nowhere to be seen.

Alex walked slowly down the road, muttering to himself. Why hadn't he thought of it a long time ago? The Earlys almost certainly had a camp. It was probably on Shrubsbury Pond. Ms. M's crash had interrupted his thinking processes. If the woman was embezzling and could afford two nice cars and one much improved home, there was almost certainly a second house, a camp. Most people, except those in the lower income classes like him and Ms. M, had one. He'd heard Colin Early talk about fishing. At the time, he'd assumed the man fished in Shrubsbury Pond; he'd pictured him there, casting for trout in his hip boots, looking like a TV commercial for beautiful Vermont. He couldn't be sure he'd actually heard anything of the kind. But it seemed as likely a next step as any, and he began the several-mile bike ride to the pond.

There was very little beach of any kind at Shrubsbury Pond, just marsh. Alex hid his bicycle in the woods, then found a rough walkway, and circled the pond, looking for Mrs. Early's Impala. He found the car on a drive not far from the road, and the camp close by the marsh bordering the lake, looking new and vulnerable in the early morning light. He found some scrub to hide in, and watched her with his binoculars. She was on the deck with a cup of coffee, her hood still tucked around her face, her face as pale as the cloudy sky. He thought she'd put on makeup, but her eye shadow was the deep circles under her eyes. She was clutching her coffee cup as if it were some kind of magical charm that could save her.

Time seemed to pass very slowly. Alex counted his shirt buttons, then the ducks scuttling round the pond. He wished he had as much patience as the woman he watched. She seemed content to sit there for the next hour, to sip coffee in the dim morning sun and wait. Finally, when it was almost time for Alex to get to his job at the museum, a green Buick pulled up. Colin Early got out and walked slowly to the deck. She watched him come. Alex tried to read her expression. Certainly, she wasn't happy, or even relieved, to see him, but she didn't seem indifferent either. Maybe, he thought, it was fear he saw on her face. He wished he could refer to a script. Or the music that filled the background on television and in the movies.

When her husband reached the deck, Cornelia Early stood up to let him kiss her cheek. They both sat down and he began talking. She studied his face as he spoke. Oh, how Alex wished he could hear. But if he moved he would be found out, and given what had happened to Ms. M, he decided to make himself stay for a quick lesson in lip reading. When Cornelia suddenly became agitated, when she clutched at her husband's arm, he thought maybe, just maybe, she'd been told about Ms. M's crash. When she implored him to do something, anything, he wondered if Bob Early was the subject. "Please, stop him, don't let him kill again." When Colin nodded slowly, and took out a pencil, Alex thought he must be writing down the amounts she'd stolen in each year of the last thirty. "No, Colin, no. It couldn't have been that much!"

Alex pinched himself. He was making it up. He had to rein in his imagination before he got lost in a script of his own. They might be talking about anything—the inefficiency of their dishwasher, their last hand of bridge with Bob and his wife, the divorce Colin had asked Cornelia for.

Colin Early left after about fifteen minutes. He was probably going to work, Alex thought. Cornelia Early went inside, and Alex went to find his bike in the woods and pedal to the museum. He had to talk to Ms. M. Even if she was sleeping all morning the way he did on unexpected holidays, he had to wake her and tell her about the morning's events.

Tasha had convinced Stuart to accompany her that morning to Early's Auto to buy a secondhand truck. Surely, Bob Early wouldn't sabotage the new truck if she brought the sheriff with her for the purchase. She intended to assure him that she harbored no suspicion of him—not a bit—and that she'd lost interest in any questions that had even remotely to do with his sister-in-law or the dead man in the pond.

The Organist Who Wore Gloves

"What do you think, Stuart? He has a red Chevy truck. I've always wanted to drive a red truck."

"It's no worse than the yellow, I suppose."

"Does it look like it's in good condition?"

"Mom, you're a senior citizen. Why can't you be more dignified?"

"What? A black truck. Gray. What would make me more dignified?"

"How about a blue car? There's a blue sedan over there that would be perfect. It probably gets good gas mileage."

"Let's look at the red truck. I haul lawn mowers and 'no parking' signs around. A blue sedan is impractical and way too serious."

Stuart sighed and opened the hood of the truck. "She looks good. We'll take a test drive and see."

Bob Early didn't talk to them until after they'd taken it out. "Stuart, Tasha. I was so sorry to hear about your accident. But I must say, Tasha, you look as if you're in good form. Is that really a broken arm, or just a sprain?"

"Fractured, the doctor said. Not much of a fracture.

It'll be as good as new in no time. I'm perfectly fit to drive, and since my wonderful yellow truck has met its end...."

"...you'll buy a red one. It's a good little truck, Stuart. In great shape, don't you think?"

"I do," Stuart said. He was tempted to ask the man about the brake lines. In fact, he was tempted to question Bob at length, but his mother had begged him to be quiet and cordial.

"I'm so grateful you had this one waiting for me, Bob. I felt badly about my lovely yellow truck."

"I know. It was very you, Tasha."

She stroked him and then the truck. "I've always told everyone I know that Early's Auto is the only place to buy. What a perfect little vehicle. It's as if it's been waiting here for me."

"And I've always told everyone I know that you're one of my favorite customers," he stroked her back.

Stuart took a deep breath and pretended that things were exactly what they seemed.

That afternoon, after a visit to Stuart's favorite

mechanic and a thorough checkup of the truck—he wasn't going to send his mother out a second time with faulty brakes—and after a short consultation with Alex, Tasha drove her new truck to Shrubsbury Pond.

Cornelia was sitting on the deck in the afternoon sun, staring at nothing. Tasha walked slowly up the path and sat down opposite her.

"I heard about your accident. Are you okay, Tasha? Is your arm truly broken?"

"It's a small fracture. How are you?"

"I knew you'd find me, that you'd figure out that this is where I'd come."

"Just a little escape?"

"Yes. Colin thought it best that I take some time away, both for my own emotional health and, I guess, to give us some time to think of what to do next."

"He must have been very upset when he found out."

"Oh, yes. He's always thought of me as someone very special, a good and virtuous woman, you know."

"Bob still doesn't know?"

"No."

"Are you missing some incriminating evidence? Is that why you were at the museum this morning?"

"Yes. Just a few more checks. You didn't keep anything out, did you?"

"No."

"I don't think it matters. They're there somewhere. I'm just a little crazy."

"Tell me how it happened, Cornelia. When did you start taking money?"

"My life of crime?" She laughed one of her strange deep chuckling laughs. "Not many weeks after I started working for Bob, Colin and I were having a tough time. He was too proud to ask his brother for a loan. It wouldn't have had to be a big loan. Just a few hundred and we'd have worked everything out. So I decided that we'd take a small loan from the company on the q.t.; we'd pay it back quickly, so no one would have to know anything. I didn't even tell Colin. I took the money and covered nicely with both Bob and my husband. No one noticed; the months passed. It had been so easy, I did it again when we had another small crisis with our house payment. Gradually, it became less and less likely I'd ever be able to pay anything back. And besides, paying it back would have called attention to all of it. That was thirty years ago. I've never had to ask Bob for a raise because I've given myself many raises.

"In my own defense, I've only taken what I needed, and what was due me. Bob's a real skinflint, you know. But he's always trusted me absolutely. He's never liked the arithmetic of business, and he's left it completely up to me. Without me, Early's Auto wouldn't be where it is today.

"When the company floundered a few years ago, I won plaudits for volunteering a cut in my salary. Next month I'm to be awarded the Volunteer of the Year award by the Jaycees. You can see that I can hardly afford to come clean now—I'd lose everything."

"Oh, Cornelia. I'm so sorry. How much have you stolen?"

"Upwards of $300,000," she said, her voice getting very small.

"Oh, Cornelia."

"I don't know who was blackmailing me, but he

began contacting me after I met the organist at the museum. The winter before last I'd started using the organ bench in the museum as a sort of bank for some of the more incriminating checks I was writing. Before then, my bank was this house, but Colin turned it into his deer camp."

"Then last winter you ran into the fellows making music in the museum?"

"Yes. And about the same time, I got the first of several threatening letters. They were put in my car at night. It made sense that it was one of them."

"Did anyone ever own up to it?"

"No."

"Did you give them any money?"

"Once. I was told to leave it in the organ bench."

"How much?"

"$10,000."

"That's a lot."

"Yes. And it was clear that whoever it was, would want more."

"But you were never sure it was one of them?"

The Organist Who Wore Gloves

"No." The two women sat silently for a few moments, watching and listening to a clutch of Canadian geese flying north. "It's spring, isn't it? I keep forgetting," Cornelia murmured.

"You're going to stay here for a while?"

"Yes, until Colin and I figure out what we should do. Or until you decide to tell your son. Or Bob. Or maybe even Adele. You won't, will you?"

"No. I'll let you and Colin try to work it out." Tasha stood up. "In the meantime, I'll be back tomorrow."

"I don't need any company."

"I'm sure you don't. You have more than enough to do, just thinking about all this. But I think you probably have more to say to me, and maybe, by tomorrow—you'll think of it."

"I've told you everything, Tasha."

"I'll see you tomorrow," Tasha said and turned to walk back down the path. "Think. Rest," she called out, and waved as she drove away in her new truck.

XXII

The lawn was sprinkled with white tents and children on a special day trip for 4-H kids. The blacksmith's hammer rang out; kids pounded new fence posts around the school garden; a team of horses clopped up the road towards High Hill with a rumbling wagon full of young people to view the surrounding countryside, all the way to Lake Memphremagog on one side and Lake Willoughby on another. The day was bright and clean; Alex was busy helping kids find the hour's activity assigned to them. Tasha was giving tours to groups in the Old Shrubsbury School Museum.

The 4-Hers arrived about ten at a time. She found herself looking forward to 11 o'clock because the adult leader in charge was Adele Early and the woman's behavior of the other day had confounded her. She'd never known her well, and she'd never quite liked her. Their most recent encounter had confirmed her view: Adele wasn't a nice person. But now that she was to have Bob Early's wife and a bunch of young people all to herself, she wanted to find out if the woman knew about Cornelia's connection to the phantom organist.

It was a well-behaved group, in fact an eerily polite group of kids. She could feel their restlessness taking form beneath the courtesy. It was like waiting for bad weather with a dark sky on the horizon. The minute Adele Early turned her attention away from them, they would explode like a bundle of firecrackers.

When they came into the music room, the questions began. "Is that a pipe organ?"

"No, Jessie. The pipes aren't real."

"They're false?"

"They're pretend."

"Pretend?"

"Yes. People wanted to pretend they were rich enough to own a pipe organ instead of a reed organ."

"Pipes are better than reeds?"

"Much."

"So this is just a reed organ. Can't the museum afford a real organ instead of a pretend one?"

"The reed organ isn't pretend. The pipes are."

"But why don't you have a pipe organ?"

"We have what people in this region had, and what they passed on to the museum."

"And the people here were dirt poor, weren't they, Ms. Mulholland?"

"Not most of them, Joey."

"So what's the difference between a pipe organ and a reed organ?"

"It's kind of like the difference between an iPhone and a prepaid phone from Walmart, isn't it Ms. M?"

"Something like that."

"Did the kids who went here care about stuff like that?"

"I don't know, but they probably did. Anyway, that organ was made decades after there were students here."

The Organist Who Wore Gloves

"Why's it here then?"

"It's part of the museum collection. People in your town and this town, people in this community, mostly had organs in the last half of the nineteenth century and the first quarter of the twentieth."

"But the students who went here never had an organ?"

"We're not sure. Maybe they did."

"If they did, they probably just sang hymns all the time."

"Oh, I don't think so," said Tasha. "There were popular songs then too."

"Can we play the organ?"

"No, I'm afraid not. No one's allowed to do that."

"Children. Children. Let's be quiet now, and let Ms. Mulholland talk about the music."

"The students here took singing lessons. They probably had instruments they could play. Like that harmonium there, and that rocking melodeon. They sound a little like an organ." She walked to the front of the group. "I like to imagine I hear them sometimes. Listen."

Everyone was quiet. They really thought they might hear something. Even Adele Early seemed to be waiting. When one of the boys whispered to another, she gave him a short light kick. They waited again. And darned if there wasn't music from somewhere. An organ playing "Sugar."

Tasha ran through the possibilities in her mind. One. She was dreaming, and no one else heard it. Except that they clearly did—their mouths were open, several of the girls were moving to the rhythm. Two. There was a recording somewhere and someone had tripped the switch. Is that what had happened the last time she heard it in the night? And what about the times before? Three. There truly was a ghost in the room, perhaps Max himself, and he was laughing at them all.

The music ended as suddenly as it had begun, and Tasha pulled herself together and smiled benignly at them all. "Let's all go upstairs now. Would you lead the way, Adele?"

They were on the fourth floor before one of the girls asked, "Ms. Mulholland, did the music we heard downstairs belong to the students in the school or the people who lived here when it was a boarding house?"

The Organist Who Wore Gloves

"Neither, Holly. It belonged to a bunch of young people who used to play in the museum in the late 1950s before there were many visitors."

"And the tune, Tasha?" asked Adele Early.

"Was a jazz tune called "Sugar," first played on an Estey organ by Fats Waller in the 1920s."

"Were you there when he played it?" asked one of the 4Hers.

Tasha sighed. "That was way before my time. Nor have I ever seen the ghosts who play here from time to time."

"Ahhhh... you made all that up, didn't you? There was a recording playing somewhere, or something."

"I dare you to explain it," said Adele Early, looking straight at her, almost laughing.

"I can't. Maybe you can."

"No, indeed. I don't know a thing about it. I've never seen an Estey before. I've never heard it played. I've certainly never heard that tune played."

Tasha looked straight into her face and couldn't tell if she was telling the truth. But why, she wondered, would the tune have happened when there was an Early (albeit by marriage) in the building, and not at some other time? As she told the kids they were excused and could go outside for the Shrubsbury Museum's famous rhubarb drink and a picnic lunch—but "Don't run down the stairs"—she thought the world seemed oddly skewed.

Later, when everyone had gone home, Tasha and Alex searched the music room, especially the Estey organ. They looked into every pretend pipe, and through the box of reeds where the instrument's voice lived. They studied the pedals, and crawled around on the floor to peer at the floor underneath the organ's carapace. Tasha became aware that someone was watching them, and turned around to look up. Adele Early was grinning at them.

"So you really didn't know where the sound was coming from?"

"I really didn't."

"Wait 'til I tell Bob about this," she said, and left, laughing.

XXIII

"Did you go see Mrs. Early this morning?" asked Alex. It was the day after the 4-H event, and he and Ms. M were off to Brattleboro again, this time in the new red truck.

"Yes. She had nothing new to say. She talked about Colin and how wonderful he was, how kind and forgiving he's been."

"I guess he'd better be. She did it for him."

"Yes. But if he didn't know…. It had to come as a terrible shock."

"What do you think they'll end up doing?"

"I presume—I don't know—that he'll work out some kind of agreement with Bob. Cornelia and Colin will pay him back over the next several years. No one will say anything to the police. That will be that."

"Do you think they've told Bob yet?"

"I don't know. I think Bob knows. He and Adele make comments that suggest they do."

"I don't understand her. What was all that stuff about the music yesterday?"

"I wish I knew. Maybe we'll know more after we talk to Noah."

"Maybe there is a ghost in the museum."

"Maybe."

"Ah, Ms. M, I didn't think I'd ever hear you say that."

"Hmmmm."

"Do you know where Noah lives?"

"I think so. He's in a wealthy part of town on a hill. Anyway, we're to meet him at the museum. Don't you think this is a wonderful truck?"

"Really wicked, Ms. M."

The day was gray and cool with clouds climbing into the sky and ground fog dancing in the valleys.

The Organist Who Wore Gloves

"Everything is beautiful today," Alex said dreamily.

"Yes, it is. This is a beautiful place, Alex."

"Even Shrubsbury."

"Yes. Even there."

"You and your husband went almost everywhere, didn't you?"

"Many continents, yes. Asia, Latin America, Europe."

"I think I would have liked Max."

"I know you would have. I did."

"I'm sorry he left you and went and died."

"Me too."

"You're pretty sure his ghost isn't around making music."

"Yes. I'm pretty sure."

"I kind of miss the yellow truck. No one but you had a yellow truck."

"I know what you mean. But red's good."

"Yeah."

They pulled into Brattleboro a few minutes early, and walked around the old Estey factory. It was one of those places—like museums and some people's homes—where you could almost see and hear the past: the yard full of workers with their lunch pails, and all around them the sounds of pounding, drilling and sawing, the music of organs everywhere, a music that grew bigger and bigger....

"Someone's playing an organ in the museum," Ms. M said.

"Wow!" said Alex. "That's some monster music."

Ms. Mulholland tried the door and pushed it open. Inside, the sound swallowed them up. At the keyboard of an Estey pipe organ that climbed nearly three stories to the ceiling, was the oldest man Alex had ever seen—tall, thin and gray with small dark eyes that snapped like fireflies. He was playing the Bach "Toccata and Fugue" the way it should be played—not on that little reed organ in the Shrubsbury Museum. It was the first time Alex, whose musical education was limited to rock, pop and a few cello solos practiced by Ms. M, realized that Max was being funny when he played this big introduction to God on that tiny pretentious organ. He liked Max more than ever.

The Organist Who Wore Gloves

He also liked Noah, because it was Noah, 101 years old, playing the organ as if he were pounding on the doors of heaven, trying to open them wide, because, at his age…well, you never know. Or so Alex speculated.

Noah Patrovsky laughed out loud when he saw them, and stopped playing. He slid across the bench carefully, stood up, and spidered his way over to them. "Hello, hello. I'm so glad to see you again, Tasha. And to meet you, young man. Alex, isn't it? If you'll follow me to my house, a splendid lunch has been prepared for us."

"You'll have to excuse me if I drive slowly," he added as they followed him to the door. "At my age, it's advisable. So just be patient, and follow me." He climbed into a red Corvette. "I like your truck," he called, fired his engine and moved out gently, smoothly.

"Oh, hey. I like that car," said Alex.

"It's an old one," said Ms. Mulholland. "I'd guess about 1995."

They made their way up narrow streets winding across lush hills and through neighborhoods of grand houses and wide green lawns, past new iris and blossoming apple trees to a grand house at the end of a long driveway.

"What do you think?" asked Noah, removing himself from the Corvette and joining them in front of the house.

"It's beautiful," said Ms. M.

Alex couldn't say a word.

"A splendid woman attends to the necessary things: lunch, dinner and the gardening," said Noah, still standing and speaking, as if he were addressing a meeting of important people. "So far, even though I've grown embarrassingly old, I can do nearly everything else for myself. In the library I have one of the antique Estey pipe organs. I try to play a bit each day. I only play the enormous monster at the museum on the days I happen to be there. You provided an occasion for me to do so, and I'm very grateful. It's a great instrument."

"We're here, Jeanette," he called out. A woman with plump cheeks and a large white smile appeared. "Bring on the feast!"

She bowed ever so slightly in his direction and left them, only to reappear minutes later when they were seated at a table in the arboretum. Immersed in greenery and exotic flowers, they sipped a perfect butternut squash soup and munched on a splendid French bread.

The trio concentrated on eating for a few minutes, moaning in gratitude for the perfection of everything, until the old man raised his hand, as if to call them to attention. "I started playing Esteys in the 1950s and became one of the factory's favored spokesmen. That's why I was here when Max Mulholland appeared. Although I had met you, Tasha, sometime before that when you and Max were passing through New York."

"I remember well. You took us to a very expensive restaurant, and then to Riverside Church where you had the key to the pipe organ and the choir loft."

"Yes, yes. A long time ago. But I'm here now, and still alive, and ready to answer any question you or your gentleman friend pose."

"I have a question," Alex said, afraid that if he waited the conversation would run to great music, organs, cellos and mathematics, and he'd dare not utter a word. "Was Max Mulholland a nice man? Or did he have a mean streak? I mean he went and left Ms. M for another woman. That wasn't nice. Then I realized when I listened to you playing the 'Toccata' that he was sort of making fun of it when he tried to play it on the little Estey at the museum."

"He had a wicked sense of humor, Alex. And you're right, he wasn't always nice. It may very well be that he devised a simple puzzle to hide a complicated secret. I don't think, however, that he would have wanted to cause a murder."

"I have one more question, Mr. Patrovsky, and then I'll just listen."

"Fire away, Mr. Churchill."

"Why are you so nice and why is Mr. Must not?"

"An excellent question. You do realize that he's old and, unlike me, not the least bit happy about being alive. That's my first answer. Secondly, he's a sourpuss." Alex laughed out loud. "But now, let's get down to it. The truth. Max was a favorite of his. He and some of the remaining Estey people thought they could bring the old factory back to life. They planned on doing so and becoming wealthy in the bargain. Max was always full of big dreams, and if he had lived, when Estey finished falling apart I'm sure he would have moved on. But not Gerald Must. Gerald was bitter, and remains bitter to this day.

The Organist Who Wore Gloves

"I haven't any notion what Max's big secret was. Since he created it in a playful mood and as a child, I think it may not have amounted to much. Not money. Not an opportunity for money. But Gerald thinks otherwise. When Max's son came through here on his way to your village of Shrubsbury, Gerald encouraged him, since he hoped the young man would find at least a small fortune there. Because he'd been a dear friend of the father, he thought that any treasure should belong to him as well as the son. I don't think Max Fox agreed.

"Now, that doesn't explain anything, does it? Certainly, Gerald Must is in no condition to travel to the Northeast Kingdom and murder someone. Even in good health, I doubt he would have done so. All I think he may have done is set the tone for Max Fox's adventure in Shrubsbury."

"Is Max's son like his father?" asked Tasha.

"He likes a challenge. He appreciated that his father had set him a musical challenge. But he doesn't have his father's charm. I think he may be a little bit of a sourpuss like his mother. And like Gerald. I think he hoped he would profit from the puzzle. I couldn't convince him that it was almost certainly something silly."

"How long ago was he here and for how long, Noah?"

"February of this year, I think. And then he took off again. I didn't know where he went or whether he was going straight to Shrubsbury."

"Do you think he was capable of trying to blackmail an embezzler?"

"I think almost anyone is capable of trying. It doesn't sound like it worked out. It would have been another way of turning Max's little game into a moneymaking venture."

After lunch, Noah took them into his library and left them there for a few minutes while he went out to have a smoke. "I know, I know. It's bad for your health," he said laughing. "Over a long, long life I've discovered that rules, of whatever kind, aren't all they're cracked up to be. The rules that affect your health. Moral rules. It's become a kind of hobby of mine to break as many as I can before I die." He pulled a pack of cigarettes from his shirt pocket and started for the garden.

The books climbed the walls on three sides like the cells of a beehive. On the fourth wall an organ stood like a monument of mahogany curlicues, topped with rows of tall shiny copper pipes. "I want you to hear something," he said when he returned. "I think it may help you think about Max's puzzle." Cautiously, he climbed onto the organ bench and took his place at the keyboard. He smiled at them almost shyly. "If it's okay with you, I'm going to play the two pieces of music that seem to be at the heart of the puzzle."

"We'd love to hear you play," Tasha said, as she and Alex settled into a couch so deep Alex thought they might get lost in it. They gazed up at him, a slender figure bending and rising, his fingers pulling out the stops and dancing across the keys, his feet tripping on the pedals.

He played notes from "The Toccata and Fugue" first, the notes climbing up as they always did to the very gates of heaven. Then, without warning, "Sugar" joined the movement, the blues blending with the spinning of the "Toccata" in a curious hybrid that was neither one nor the other, but both. There he sat, Noah Patrovsky, who claimed to have breached a century, turning the music of the phantom organist into celebration.

"Oh, man," said Alex as they drove away from Noah's house. "What a house! All those books. Did you see all those books? If it were me, I would have a room full of computer stuff, and another with pianos and guitars. Maybe an organ. I'm still not sure about organs. But a cello, of course," he smiled at Ms. M. "I'd make a special bedroom for my mom. I'd have a garden for my mom in the middle of my house like Noah's...."

Alex chattered all the way to Lake Morey. Then, just before he nodded off for an afternoon nap, he murmured. "What do you think, Ms. M? Maybe I have an old soul. My favorite people in the whole world are old people."

XXIV

The next day was a perfect spring day. The cemetery was full of robins and swallows piecing together new nests. A hummingbird, just returned from some fantastic migration, impatiently buzzed around still-budding flowers. A bluebird explored a favorite birdhouse at the edge of the cemetery where Ms. M and Alex met at the hidden stone for a strategy session. She'd brought a meal of potato salad, bologna sandwiches and lemonade for them.

"Let's talk about the dead man, Alex. We still don't know who he was."

"Yeah. But Asa Parker seemed pretty sure he was the one who stayed with him."

"But we haven't been able to discover anything about him. It's like he never existed."

"So the name was probably an alias," said Alex.

"It would seem so. No one but Asa Parker has been able to match up the picture with somebody they knew. Even Parker wasn't 100 percent certain. There was no wallet or any form of identification on him. They haven't found any fingerprints on any of their databases that match his. His clothing suggests that he earned a substantial living. His shirt was fashionable and expensive. His shoes were costly. His hands didn't look like those of someone who does manual labor. He didn't have a ring. He was in his early thirties and in good physical condition. He may have exercised at a gym. And, Alex, he wasn't a smoker so the Camel cigarettes weren't his."

"So that's pretty much it?" asked Alex.

"Yes."

"So he's a thirty-something–year-old, probably a businessman or something like that," he summed it up. "What do we know about how he was killed?"

"He was shot in the back of the head. He was either close enough to the edge to fall in, or the killer pushed his body into the pond. It wouldn't have taken much strength to push the body in if he was already on the dock."

"So Cornelia Early could have done it."

"She has the best motive if he was the blackmailer."

"I have a couple of questions for you, Ms. M. Why would the killer have taken away all his identification? Where would he have put it?"

"I suppose the obvious answer is that if we knew who the dead man was, we might figure out who the murderer was. As to where the ID has got to, I imagine it was burned or tossed into a landfill somewhere."

"Did Sheriff Mulholland look in trash cans around the museum?"

"We must assume so. That's pretty basic."

They sat quietly eating. Ms. M opened a container full of ginger snaps. "Now I want you to think about another question. Why wasn't he wearing his camel hair coat? He was outside. The nights were still very cold."

"Maybe it wasn't his coat."

"Why would the murderer have put someone else's coat in the water with him?"

"Like it was an afterthought to make it look like he was the other guy!" Alex guessed.

"To make it look like it was Max Fox instead of Joel McPherson?"

"Yeah."

"And if they put the key and the medallion in the pocket, that would even more nearly indicate that it was Max."

"You know, Ms. M. I keep thinking Max Fox might have offed Joel McPherson."

"As Hercule Poirot said, 'Let's make use of our little gray cells.' That's a very interesting idea, Alex. I hope it's not the case. But let's keep thinking all the same, no matter what the outcome.

"Besides, we should lie low for a bit. If we don't, my son will put me away somewhere and your mother will lock you up. Let's keep quiet this afternoon and do a lot of thinking."

XXV

Tasha was in her house that night, playing George Gershwin songs on her cello when her music was interrupted by someone playing "Sugar" on the Estey organ. She stopped and shook her head in disbelief. Why was he back? What was he looking for?

The moon made the lawn bright between her house and the museum, so she had no need to turn on her flashlight. She went in through the kitchen door as quietly as she could, and stood listening as the organist struggled to put all the sound he could into the music. She found a place to hide in the shadows of the next room, and when the musician quit, she called out,

"Max Fox. Is that you? Joel McPherson? Why are you still haunting this place?"

No answer.

She tried again: "One of you is dead. Is the other one the killer? I hope you're not hoping to find money at the end of Max Mulholland's rainbow. I'm sure there's nothing. Is that why you're threatening Cornelia Early? Are you hoping to come up with some money, somehow?"

No one answered her. She heard the kitchen door open, and close. By the time she got there, as fast as she was, there was no one.

He must not have found the answer to the puzzle. Why else would he still be playing the organ? And if he was still looking for a cache of money then, perhaps, he had killed Joel McPherson or whoever the dead man was. But she didn't want to believe that Max Fox, son of Max Mulholland, once her husband, was guilty of murder.

Tasha and Alex were planting the last of the pansies around the museum early in the morning when Serendipity came over. She stood there for a while, just watching them, then asked in a loud voice: "I'm not sure I want to know, but what was going on over here last night? At about 11, 11:30, I heard someone playing the Estey full out. Did you go over to find Max?"

"There is no Max Mulholland, Sera."

"Did you see the organist?"

"No."

"Who on earth did you think it was?"

"Max's son, Sera. Most likely. Max is dead. He died many years ago."

"Such foolishness. He's not dead. He was never dead, unless he died last night. He didn't, did he?"

"Of course not. Why didn't you come looking for him and see for yourself?"

"Just fear, Tasha. Plain old unadulterated fear."

"You were never afraid of Max before. Why now?"

"Because he might be a ghost. I don't relish odd people at the best of times. Dead ones even less."

Tasha sighed. The woman was clearly impossible, so she changed the subject. "I tried to ask you this the last time we talked, Sera, and you didn't seem to remember anything about it. Do you recall Max hiding something in the museum and making a riddle of it?"

"Hiding something. Let me think. If he did, and I really don't remember, it would have something to do with music and some of the weird old noisemakers here, wouldn't it?"

"Yes, it would."

"I don't remember anything about a riddle. But I can be of some help to you. I know some scandalous things about the principals in this mystery that you don't."

"Tell away," Alex said, ducking his head and plying his garden spade when Ms. M shushed him. "But he's right, I guess," Tasha said. "It's not very nice—but tell away."

Serendipity laughed happily. "Good," she said. "The boy will turn you into someone more like the rest of us!" She sat down on the ground in the traditional Sukhasana yoga position, her dress spread around her. "First of all, I suppose you know that the Early boys are both in love with Cornelia and always have been. I mean she married Colin, but she and Bob, especially lately, have been spending time together. Which, as you can imagine, has enraged poor Adele."

The Organist Who Wore Gloves

"My goodness. I had no idea." Tasha looked over at Alex and wondered if she should send him somewhere out of earshot. He grinned at her and shrugged.

"Yes. Isn't it wonderful? Our own soap opera. Bob has been sneaking out of the house at all hours, and Adele is furious."

"Adele knows he's seeing Cornelia?"

"He tells her there's no one, but she knows...."

"I didn't know you and Adele were friends."

"Yes, indeed. And I've learned a lot from her."

"Does she agree with you that Maxwell is still alive, and that his ghost is haunting us?"

"She does."

"And why do you, why does she, think Max is haunting the museum?"

"She thinks he's out to avenge his friend who died. Whoever that poor drowned boy was."

"And do you, does she, have any idea of who the murderer is?"

"Not so I would say, dear Tasha. No. I leave that to you and your partner." Serendipity rose up from the ground like the earth goddess Erde Tasha remembered from a Wagnerian opera years before, and headed back to her house. They watched her go.

"She's full of peculiar ideas. Cornelia and Colin have always been everyone's idea of the perfect couple, deeply in love, constant companions—all of it. And Bob has always taken care of his younger brother. As far as I know an affair between Bob and Cornelia is almost as unlikely as Max becoming a ghost."

She and Alex planted the last few pansies, patting down the sweet soil, neither saying a word until Alex remembered a question he'd been wanting to ask: "Ms. M, does Colin Early smoke?"

"I don't know."

"Does Bob Early?"

"I don't know that either. I know Cornelia used to."

"Hmmmm."

"I think I'd better visit Cornelia again. Maybe later this morning."

The Organist Who Wore Gloves

"Yeah, you'd probably better."

"And you, what are you going to do?"

"I'm not sure."

"Just be careful, Alex. Please, be very, very careful."

"I will. I promise. You too, Ms. M."

XXVI

Alex didn't really know what to do next. It seemed to him that the Earlys should be investigated, but he didn't know how to go about it. However, he had one more hunch. He called Coker who was home playing Star Wars: The Force Unleashed II.

"I need you, Coke. I want to do some investigating, and only you can help me. You know how to talk to Zoe. I get close to her and I get weird. I can't speak. I break out in a sweat. Come on, man. It doesn't need to take a long time."

Coker sighed. "Okay. But let's keep it short. I'm at a really critical place in this game."

A half hour later he and Alex found Zoe tending the museum store. She'd listened when Lori advised her to wear clothes that were looser and didn't cling so to her "quite wonderful figure." But as far as Alex was concerned, she could have been naked. She was just that sexy. He was immediately rendered mute. But he'd given Coker instructions and Coker, who seemed utterly unaffected by her, was perfectly articulate.

"Zoe, can we ask you some more questions about Joel McPherson?"

"Of course. I'll tell you anything I know. Just remember it's unlikely to be important or I would have told you about it already."

"What did you think of him? Did you talk to him?"

"Yeah, sometimes he'd come home and we'd sit on the porch and talk. He'd been lots of places and he'd tell me all about them. He was cute, but, of course, he was too old for me."

Yeah, thought Alex. Like you are for me, but jeeze....

"Did he ever mention his friend, Max?" asked Coker.

"I don't remember the name."

"Did he mention Brattleboro?" Alex interrupted, and turned so red when he heard his own voice, he wished he hadn't.

"Yes. He had friends there. Can you believe it, he had a friend who was 101 years old?"

"Oh, man," said Coker.

"He said the guy could beat him at pool."

"Yeah, he probably could," murmured Alex.

"What did he say about his work here?"

"He said he had an opportunity, he just had to be patient. He was expecting a bundle."

"What did he tell you he did for a living?" Alex blurted out.

"Well, of course, he was doing some kind of work at Early's. But that wasn't his real job. He said he was an entrepreneur."

"Oh, jeeze. Did he smoke?"

"I don't know. I didn't smell it on him."

"Did you like him? Tell us what he was like."

"Yeah, I did. But I don't have great judgment where men are concerned. Like I think Alex is the cutest boy, but I'm not sure he's a gentleman. He's always blushing when I'm around."

The Organist Who Wore Gloves

Alex felt himself sink into the ground and disappear. As he gradually regained consciousness, Zoe's voice re-emerged: "I think Joel was probably a no-good-nick. He wore a money belt. Guys who wear money belts in my short experience are nearly always bad guys."

"You know, it makes no sense," said Coker. "A guy who rides a bike instead of a car. Rents a room. How did he get to work anyway? He didn't ride the bike, did he?"

"No. He had a car."

"Omygod. What kind? Where did it go?" Alex nearly shouted.

"I guess he drove it away when he left. I dunno."

"But what was it? What year? What color? What make?"

"I know absolutely nothing about cars except that some are groovier than others. This one was very ordinary. Tan. Vermont license plates. I don't know anything else."

"Coker. We've gotta find that car!" said Alex. He turned to Zoe again, and for moments forgot that she was a good looking girl, or a girl at all. "Can't you tell us anything about it? Was it messy inside? Was it clean?

Did it look old on the inside?"

"It wasn't messy. He drove me to school once. I thought it was kind of stale inside. You know, like maybe it was rented."

"How are we going to find that car, Coker?"

"I don't know, dude. We're just kids and no one's going to talk to us. What, we walk into Hertz and ask if someone neglected to return a beige car this month because they were dead? You think they're gonna tell us anything?"

"If he never returned it, or if he never rented it and it's his, and it's just been hidden away—someone could have hidden it, you know, like the murderer, maybe—there has to be a way to find it, Coker."

"Where are you going to look?"

"You haven't seen any junked cars lately, have you?"

"Nah. Maybe a black one. No brown."

"If he came from Brattleboro, that's probably where he rented it. So if you killed some guy and you didn't want anyone to be able to identify him, where would you hide the car?"

The Organist Who Wore Gloves

"Jeeze. I dunno."

"If you were a car salesman, maybe you'd hide it in the middle of a lot of other cars. That *CSI* thing I told you about before."

"Yeah, that makes sense."

"So, how about a long bike ride to Early's Auto?"

XXVII

Tasha hid her truck in the woods near Shrubsbury Pond. She wanted to surprise Cornelia. Wary, remembering that someone related to Cornelia had probably cut her brake lines, she left a note at the museum that explained where she'd gone if she didn't return.

She approached Cornelia's house from the other side of the pond, skirting the wettest parts of the marsh until she found a board walkway that the Earlys and their neighbors had built years before. She walked softly, an elderly woman with one arm in a sling, listening to every quack of the newly arrived mallards, the bass burble of what must be at least a quartet of bullfrogs, the slap of a line as a fishing fly hit the brown water, the lapping of the sluggish current against the side of Colin Early's moored boat. The back of the house was as closed up as if it were still winter and not a day almost as warm as summer, as if the crisp vinyl clapboards formed a shell and something might be growing inside, invisible from the outside.

In the end, the only way to approach the front of the house was up the same path she'd taken the last time she'd come. Anyone in the house would be able to see her. So, she stayed at the back and found a good place to squat behind a bunch of cedars with wet feet. If nothing happened soon, she thought, as her legs began to ache, she'd stiffen and turn into an ornament like the other creatures half-hidden among the young cattails: an arching heron, a leaping trout and a fake fisherman with a net poised to catch it. She wasn't sure who she expected to see approaching the house. Maybe Max Fox. Somehow, she thought he must be around, and if he was hidden somewhere, where better than here?

The air began to thicken as the sun climbed higher in the sky. There wasn't a breeze; everything was so still it seemed barely alive. The tree branches hung heavily; from where she crouched they might have been painted on the sky. From inside the house, she heard music: Fats Waller playing "Sugar," Alberta Hunter singing. She and Alex had googled the music weeks ago and discovered that sometime after Waller played it solo on the Estey, he played it again on the same organ and Hunter sang.

It wasn't long before Tasha stretched and stood up. Too stiff to stay where she was, she decided to move to the shed, trying not to dance to the music as she went. Her sling felt damp and soiled. The shed door had been left ajar and she ducked inside to wait again, this time in a cool darkness fragrant with compost. On the wall opposite, garden implements were lined up, hanging, leaning, ready for their mistress's hand. She remembered that it was spring and Cornelia was a first rate gardener.

Alberta sang on. Twice, a third time. The music finally ended and a man came onto the deck. Squinting through the crack left by the partly open door, she couldn't quite make him out and she waited while her eyes adjusted to the light. He pulled on a shirt and began buttoning it, then turned away from Tasha's inquiring gaze to answer a question from someone inside with a "Yes. I'm on my way." He tucked his shirt in. She waited patiently—hoping, perhaps, for Max Fox to reveal himself. Of course, it might just as well be Colin Early, getting ready for a late beginning to the day.

The Organist Who Wore Gloves

Cornelia appeared at the door and looked up at him. "Be careful," she said, reaching up to straighten his collar. He put his arms around her and drew her close. Passionately, thought Tasha, glad that Alex wasn't here. Then he turned, and she drew a sharp breath. "My God," she thought, "Sera was right." Bob Early pulled away from Cornelia and turned and looked out across the water. He scanned the pond, pausing to gaze at the shed. "I'd better be off," he said. "It'll all be okay soon. Don't worry. Just keep away from the old woman and the kid."

Bob Early drove away, leaving Cornelia looking after him blankly, and Tasha trying to think through what she must still do. The affair wasn't her business, she thought, feeling a flash of envy: how she would love one last affair in her own life—how perfectly lovely that would be. But for the moment, her only business was to figure out who murdered who and why.

In the meantime, should she wait to see if Cornelia had more lodgers, or more visitors? Should she confront the woman? Again? What if she came out to garden? Surely, she'd look inside her garden shed. What if Adele showed up? Or nearly as bad—Serendipity?

Hardly had Bob disappeared when Colin came. Of course it would be him. He strode up the walkway as if he were certain of a warm welcome. The sliding windows were pushed back again and out Cornelia came, her face flushed with welcome. Tasha stared in wonderment. Not a moment's hesitation, not a stutter. She greeted him with all the passion she'd shown Bob when she said goodbye.

When they'd gone inside, she thought about leaving. It wasn't comfortable in the garden shed. It made her skin feel thick and flaky. Her broken arm hurt. But wasn't it possible that Cornelia would have more visitors? Someone she hadn't thought of? What a complicated life the woman led! She settled in and waited.

Nearly an hour passed before Colin left, smoothing his hair and straightening his tie, late for an appointment, she thought. She waited to see what would happen next. She was growing used to the shed. She felt part of the damp soil, as if she were one of the tender green plants emerging from it. She wasn't sure Cornelia's peculiar love life had anything to do with the murder. She wondered how she would talk to Alex about it.

Another half hour passed and another car pulled

into the parking area. Serendipity's Rolls. Tasha shook her head in disbelief and watched as the large woman in purple wandered up the walk, admiring wild things and tugging at a bit of budding plant here and there. She walked onto the deck and knocked on one of the glass doors.

"Sera! So good to see you. Do come in. Would you like some tea?"

"I would, I would."

Now, thought Tasha, I must go up to the sliding doors and listen. I must find out what they're talking about. If they come out onto the deck to drink their tea, I'll have to climb over the railing and hide around the corner of the house. But, it could just be worth it.

Moments later, she was at the door, listening to the two women talk in the kitchen. "Have you made up your mind what you'll do next?" asked Sera.

"I'm not sure. There might not be a problem except for Tasha and the boy. If only they didn't fancy themselves detectives."

"They don't know very much, Connie."

"But they suspect a great deal."

"Maybe Bob could do something about it."

"He's trying. But the last time he almost killed someone. Stop them, but don't kill anyone. Wouldn't you think that would be possible, Sera?"

"I would think so."

Another car pulled up and Tasha went over the railing to crouch in the mud on the side of the house. Squatting there, feeling it ooze up around her, her skin cooling in the deep shade and the vinyl of the house pressing against her broken arm, she hoped almost desperately that Cornelia and her guests would come out onto the deck where she could hear them. No matter what, eventually she'd have to make her way through the marsh and back to the path. She imagined the mud seeping into her shoes and her feet growing heavy. She worried how she'd keep the shining vinyl seat in the red truck clean. She longed for a shower.

She couldn't see him from where she was hiding, even when he was at the door, but it was a man. Of that she was certain. He and Cornelia murmured something to each other at the door. He couldn't be her lover or her husband come back; the car was one she didn't know. They went inside, and she heard the glass doors rumble closed. All she could hear were indistinct voices. Not a word. It might have been a good idea, she thought later, to have stayed to see if she could recognize the last visitor when he left, but it seemed to her then that it was an even better idea to go look at his car and get back to her own truck. She could wait for him on the road and find out who he was. Best of all, she'd be out of the mud.

Sitting in her truck on the morning's newspaper, caked mud drying, her clothes stiffening, she waited for the strange blue car parked near the pond to move. Twenty minutes passed before Serendipity came out and drove her Rolls away. It was another twenty before a man in a smart gray suit came striding down the walk to the car. She'd seen him not many weeks before when he was considerably older, when his step was mincing and he doddered, not strode. Gerald Must. Now what was she to make of that?

XXVIII

Alex and Coker had ridden the miles to Early's Auto with only a few of Ms. M's chocolate chip cookies to sustain them. They were tired, but Alex was excited. If they could find the car in the Early's lot, they'd know Bob Early was mixed up in the murder. The boys walked up and down the rows of cars, stopping to examine automobiles of every shade of brown. Was the interior only lightly used? Was there anything to suggest that the car was a rental from Brattleboro? They were studying a used beige Chevy when Bob Early surprised them.

"You fellows looking for a car? You're a little young, but if you wait around a few years I'll be happy to help you." He smiled the dimpled smile that he used when he was selling cars. His eyes danced. He exuded charm.

The Organist Who Wore Gloves

"We were inspired by your talk at school, Mr. Early. We wanted to come and see what you do firsthand," Coker said.

"Do you mind if we just look?" asked Alex.

"No. Feel free. Just don't get in anyone's way."

"Yeah. We'll be nearly invisible, we won't be long...." said Coker.

"We're looking for a brown car, Mr. Early," Alex interrupted. "Coker's mom has been talking about getting a brown car."

"She's kind of conservative," added Coker.

"No particular model?"

"I dunno. She doesn't know much about cars. I'd rather have something cool like a silver Toyota, but not her."

"She doesn't want it new," added Alex.

"Yeah, but not too old either. Used but not used up, you know."

"Hmmmm. Well, there aren't too many used brown cars on the lot right now. But you're welcome to look, guys." Bob Early turned and walked away.

"Well, that takes care of that," said Alex when he'd gone. "He knows what we're looking for and he's not worried because he knows it's not here." He kicked a tire and went over to a bench to sit.

"Yeah. I guess you're probably right. Are you sure? You don't know he had anything to do with the murder, Alex."

"I'm sure. We've gotta think of a way to fool him and find that car."

"You think there's another car lot somewhere?"

"I dunno. What do you think?"

"Nah! We'd know about it."

"You know what I'd do with a car like that?"

"What?"

"I'd put it in Shrubsbury Pond."

Bob Early was no longer smiling. His face was grim and his soft boyish features had hardened. The kids were mostly just a nuisance. He was especially irritated because he was used to solving real problems, not crap like this. But the kids had already found the bicycle and he didn't know what to do about them. He certainly wasn't going to try anything as risky as he had with Tasha Mulholland and her silly yellow truck. She and her little assistant didn't give up easily.

He sat at his desk and doodled on a half-filled-in contract. For the moment, he could just wait until they bored themselves to death looking. It was unlikely they'd find the guy's car. But he had to protect Cornelia and her tiresome husband, his tiresome brother Colin. Cornelia and his business were the two things he loved most in the world. If only Tasha would leave well enough alone. She made everything so much worse. Max's son had been a fortune hunter and a troublemaker. That he was dead was a great public benefit. If only she knew that.

The phone rang. Bob glanced at the caller ID and picked up. "Hello, darling. What's happening?"

He listened, his free hand tightening into a fist. "Yeah, well you knew Colin would be there. I'm sure you gave him what he wanted. Who else?

"Oh, shit. You're kidding me. That old bastard. He wants money, doesn't he? Did you get his phone number? Where's he staying?"

Listening to the tearful, fading voice on the other end of the line, he shook his head sadly. "Don't worry, darling. He doesn't know anything and he can't hurt you. It will all be okay. You just rest."

"Ah, Ms. M! What if someone had seen you? You weren't careful at all."

She smiled fondly at him. "Alex, I was. No one had the vaguest idea I was there. The only harm I suffered was muddiness. And a deeper state of what's become an ongoing state of confusion. Now what's this idea you have about the dead man's car?"

XXIX

Alex's mother was astonished that he was listening to old-time jazz and classical organ instead of the Beastie Boys. She was grateful—but suspicious. He danced at his chores to the one, and sat pondering with the other. She knew he loved Ms. M, but this was ridiculous.

"Since when," she asked, "do you listen to that music? And why?"

"Did you know you can put the two together and it sounds okay because they're both in the same key and have the same time sign?"

"No. How do you know that? I don't believe it."

"The old organist Ms. M and I visited in Brattleboro did it. I heard it with my own ears. He put them together and it worked. Just a little of it, but it did."

"Amazing. At 101 I'm surprised he could do anything."

"Yeah. He was amazing...." Alex's voice trailed off as he walked outside and sat down in one of the green metal chairs by the door.

"You know, Mom?" he called from outside as she began washing the dinner dishes in the kitchen sink. "It's probably not just the music that can be put together. Bach played around with letters and words too."

She had no idea what kind of response he wanted, so she didn't say anything.

"'Sugar,' 'Toccata.' If you put those two words together." He was gazing out across the pasture to the woods filling with shadows. "Mom, I have to go see Ms. M."

"Now? Why now? It's almost dark."

"I won't be long. I just have to check and see about a sugar bowl. I'll only be half an hour or so."

"Oh, really Alex! I want you back here before it gets dark. That means in less than an hour. If you're not

The Organist Who Wore Gloves

here, you're grounded this weekend."

"Thanks, Mom," Alex shouted as he ran to his bike and jumped on it almost as if it were a horse and he was off to warn someone of something impending: flood, fire, or earthquake.

Tasha heard him running up the stairs. Gusty barked. Winky hid. Ms. M opened the door and he burst inside. "Is there a sugar bowl in the museum kitchen?"

"There are several."

"Is there an Italian one?

"I don't know. I've never cared much about sugar bowls."

"Can we go look?"

"Now?"

"Yes."

"Okay. Let me get a sweater. It's cold out there. You come too, Gusty."

The three of them moved quickly across the lawn, towards the darkening museum—Alex nearly running, then slowing to keep pace with Ms. M's stride, Gusty running first one direction, then the other and barking with joy because no matter what was going on it was exciting to run in the evening with a boy.

Inside, they went straight to the cupboard in the corner of the room where fine china of other eras lined the shelves. "It'll be on the fourth shelf down," Alex said. Ms. M looked at him incredulously. "Because that's how many times the 'Sugar' phrases fit into the 'Toccata.'"

She pulled out a pretty sugar bowl in Willowware, took the lid off, and stared into it. It was empty.

"I'm sorry, Alex. It was a good idea. Do you want to look at the rest of the sugar bowls?"

Alex shrugged, and they began looking through one bowl after another, none of them Italian. "Oh God, Ms. M," he said, looking out the window. "It's almost dark. I'm supposed to be home in minutes."

"Run. Ride, Alex. We'll talk tomorrow. And be careful. Have her phone me if you're in trouble," she called out as he set off out the door.

XXX

Tasha wrote to Noah Patrovsky reporting Gerald Must's apparent involvement in the murder of the organist. Was Must the other man with the organist Alex saw that night? Or was it someone else altogether? She hoped that Noah could give her an answer.

Alex joined her for lunch and they took a picnic out to the burial stone. Ms. M laid a checkered tablecloth across it and set out a big blue thermos of lemonade, some paper cups, and their favorite sandwiches—lox and cream cheese for her and peanut butter and strawberry jam for him. The trees and bushes had greened up since their last meeting, and robins were everywhere, looking for worms.

"I'm not sure what we should do next. Do you have any ideas?"

"I want to find out if there's a brown car in Shrubsbury Pond."

"I don't think you'll get Stuart to go dredging for one, but he might look for a place where a car could have gone in. I don't want you boys searching the pond. If Bob is already aware of what you're doing, he might show up. Someone, probably one of the Early clan, is a murderer. Stay away from the pond. We'll figure out how to get Stuart to go look."

"Yeah. I know. I expected you to say that," sighed Alex.

"I think you and I should visit Serendipity. Why was she at Cornelia's yesterday? But maybe we shouldn't ask her outright. We should approach her more cleverly than that. You're the perfect person to throw her off, you know."

"Who, me?"

"You. You can charm her."

"How? Me?"

"You. You've charmed me many times."

"Yeah, but she's…. scary."

The Organist Who Wore Gloves

"Just ask her how she is. Compliment her clothing. Her hair. Her general appearance. Ask questions about the house. About her pottery. Make her think you profoundly admire her."

And so he did.

There they were, on the patio behind the house, sipping iced tea and root beer, listening to a long disquisition by Serendipity on the craft of throwing pots. Alex nodded, his eyes wide to keep them open, his laugh loud and infectious. It took a very long time, it seemed to him, for Ms. M to ask the question.

"I noticed your car at Cornelia's camp yesterday, Sera. How did she seem to you?"

"Oh, still tired. But better."

"I didn't know you knew her so well, you'd visit her there."

"Oh, yes. Her, Adele, Colin, Bob. All of them."

Tasha took a big breath. She might as well ask the question. "How about Gerald Must?"

"You were watching Cornelia's camp, weren't you? You evil woman."

"Not as evil as Mr. Must surely."

"Gerald Must isn't evil. He's just—"she looked for the perfect word"—avaricious."

"Avaricious?" Alex noted the word—surely a word for the day.

"Yes. You know, greedy. He wants some money for his silence about Cornelia's indiscretions."

"He'd tell who? Bob? Surely, Bob must have guessed at everything by now. The local gendarmes? If Bob doesn't press charges, does it matter?"

"Cornelia's alleged indiscretions are much more impressive than you seem to have guessed."

"Did she kill the organist?"

"I don't know, but there's a perception out there that she could have. And that alone could be worth quite a few dollars."

"Oh, my. Shrubsbury is suddenly rife with avaricious people."

"Of course. It's the best way to be."

"Since you know so many things, do you know if the organist was blackmailing Cornelia as well?"

The Organist Who Wore Gloves

"I don't know if it was him any more than Cornelia does."

"Is she going to try to pay off Gerald Must?"

"I can't tell you. She was going to talk it over with Colin."

'Let's get back to you, my dear. Were you at Cornelia's for any special reason?"

"Oh, no. Just to show my concern for her."

"Hmmmm. Another question. I'm just curious. Would you rather see Cornelia with Colin or Bob?"

"She doesn't have to choose, you know. The men seem to appreciate the present arrangement."

"Which one are you interested in?"

"Oh, Tasha. Really. The truth is the only one I want is Max Mulholland."

"Dead as a doornail."

"Not. He's not, I tell you," she said, rising with a flourish. "You've heard him play the last few days. You know the organist is dead; we all saw the body. So who's playing, if not Max himself?"

"I don't know," Tasha said quietly.

"You know none of us can really play, not that well. Not Cornelia. Certainly not Colin or Bob. Adele has no musical sense at all. Nor do I."

"Alex and I believe there were two men, the organist, and another, hanging around the museum on some nights. One of them is dead. The other is still alive. They may be Max Fox and someone called Joel McPherson. We're not sure which man is the dead man."

"How ever did you come up with that idea?"

"Alex saw two, and Cornelia between them. Cornelia agrees there are two."

Everyone was quiet, thinking about the conundrum—one man or two. One dead, one alive?

"Maybe one of them—Max Fox or Joel—is Gerald Must," said Alex.

"My head hurts," said Ms. M.

"If you believe, as I do, that Max himself is hanging around, it will all seem simple," Sera said. "I tell you what, let's gang up on whoever it is, even if it's Max. The next time someone plays the organ, I'll come too.

The Organist Who Wore Gloves

We'll catch the culprit. Makeup be damned! I'm extraordinary in whatever guise I appear."

Alex and Ms. M both smiled. Yes, you are, they wanted to shout, but it seemed rude.

XXXI

Dear Tasha and Alex, I wouldn't put it past Gerald Must to blackmail someone. He's a nasty rascal of an old man, and greedy besides. I'm afraid I can't speak to any of the particulars. He's probably acquainted with several of the people at Shrubsbury. He was, after all, a friend of Max's when the two of you were married, and before Max's death. I know the Early brothers visited here at least once. I don't know that Cornelia was ever here, but I suppose she could have been.

I gather you've had no luck answering Max's riddle. I had hoped my little musical offering would help. I'm sure it can't be that difficult, although I have no idea whether or not its solution would help you solve the murder of the organist.

I enjoyed having the two of you to lunch very much.

The Organist Who Wore Gloves

It would be lovely if you could come and visit again soon. Very soon. I don't expect to live on too much longer.

It sounds as if you're having an interesting spring. Be careful, both of you. Shrubsbury seems to be a dangerous place to live.

Cheers, Noah Patrovsky

Sheriff Stuart Mulholland examined the shore of Shrubsbury Pond on every side, and saw no reason to look further. There was no sign that a car had been pushed into the water.

Because they were at a loss about what to do next, Ms. M and Alex looked forward to another appearance by the organist, and the participation of Serendipity Hamilton in the investigation. The problem was getting Alex to the museum in the middle of the night if the organist should appear. Ms. M had an aversion to lying to his mother, and so she told her outright that Alex had been invited by Serendipity, along with herself, to explore the reality of ghosts. She didn't know exactly when. Sera claimed she had no idea when the apparition might appear, if it was an apparition and not Max himself. For her part, Tasha found the idea an educational one. She'd heard Alex and Coker wonder aloud whether there were ghosts. Alex was intrigued by Sera's planned event. Ms. M was sure the boy would see through any performance initiated by Sera Hamilton.

Apart from its educational value, maybe they'd finally find out who the latest musician was.

It was a moonless night when the organist played again. Ms. M was reading a murder mystery by Louise Penny. The story took place only a few miles north, on the other side of the Canadian border in the Eastern Townships. She knew it was ridiculous to look for help in a fictional mystery, no matter how near it was geographically, but she hoped for some kind of clue to her own dilemma. Penny's detective, after all, was a professional policeman, not some old lady and a kid.

Inspector Gamache had just uncovered an important lead when the organist began playing "Sugar." Tasha called Alex. "He's here!" she said, and hung up. She slipped on a jacket and shoes, grabbed her flashlight, but didn't turn it on, and headed for the museum. Serendipity was close behind. She went to the kitchen door while Sera, in keeping with their plan, stopped at the main door, which already stood open as if the ghost were welcoming her. The ghost couldn't get past them unless he truly was a ghost. There were no other doors.

Apparently unaware of their presence, the organist played on. The two women had synchronized their watches. At exactly the same moment, Sera entered the big door at the front, and Ms. M unlocked and pushed into the kitchen door. They both stayed, blocking the exits, waiting for the music to end, because it hadn't. The organist continued to play.

"Sugar, I never cheat on sugar, 'Cause I'm too sweet on my sugar, That sugar baby of mine," Tasha sang under her breath as the music ended.

There was a sound like the organ bench being scraped across the floor. Someone moved, then walked, not to the front door or the kitchen, but somewhere that seemed undefined—to the hallway, up the stairs, to the next room…. Neither woman could have said. But both stayed at their stations. This time the phantom wouldn't escape.

Tasha and Serendipity Hamilton were ready for any eventuality. If the phantom didn't try to make an escape through the doors, there were several possibilities. He was waiting until they were off guard to make his escape. He was a recording triggered by some other unseen presence. (The trick was to find the person punching the recording machine.) He was a ghost and if they called him on it, he would have to make some kind of gesture to affirm his presence.

Alex bicycled up by the kitchen door and took Tasha's place so she could begin to explore the museum, looking for the ghostly musician, whoever he was. She headed for the stairs and moved up them as quietly as she could. She could be heard, of course, but the sound she made was obscured by another that she simulated with a bit of a broom—the trees tossing in a breeze, a sound she'd practiced at home. On the second floor she stopped and listened before she moved on. She heard the scrape of chalk on slate, and moved towards Timothy Evensong's room. They'd never been so close to finding out who the organist was. Or at least who this incarnation of the man was.

She reached the doorway and stared across at the dark shadow there, merging with the blackness of the room. "Hullo, who are you?"

A cloaked figure whirled around and stared at her, then dropped the globe where it did a quick little bounce and began rolling across the floor. Tasha fell to her knees to stop it. Her broken arm slammed into a table leg, and she groaned aloud as the organist headed for the first floor. "He's coming down," she managed to shout. She heard noises at the front door. She replaced the ball on the table carefully, and plunged down the steps, reaching the doorway just as Alex did. There, on the front porch, they found Sera Hamilton perched triumphantly on top of the organist.

"You were right," she shouted. "This is no ghost! And it's certainly not Max Mulholland."

Alex shined his light onto the dark figure struggling for breath under Serendipity's bulk.

Sera reached over and pulled the cape from his head, but this particular phantom at least was no he.

It was Adele Early.

"Oh, my," murmured Sera. "I hope I'm not hurting you, dear," and she rose like a great bird above the supine Adele who rolled out from under her to sit on the stone porch, glaring at them all, an angry Rumpelstiltskin of a woman.

"Adele, what in the name of all that's holy, are you doing?" asked Ms. Mulholland.

"I'm helping my fool of a husband, that's what I'm doing," Adele snapped. "My God, how much do you weigh, Sera?"

"I thought your 'fool of a husband' was a car salesman," Ms. M snapped back, "not a phony organist."

"None of your business what I weigh!" growled Sera. "Where's Bob?"

"He's not here. I'm his little messenger from the Great Beyond."

"Why?" asked Ms. M.

Alex, being a kid, just stared at them all. Grown ups! thought Alex. Egad, they're strange.

"Because Bob wanted to continue the haunting started by Max Fox. He learned from Cornelia that you thought there were two men, and he wanted you to keep believing that—to believe even that one of them was the killer of the other. He's been playing a recording of 'Sugar,' and another of 'The Toccata and Fugue.' He put a poem on the slate globe."

"Why would he want us to believe there were two men?"

"Because you'll think that the one still living is the suspect instead of his brother or his beloved Cornelia."

"But why would you do this for Bob, Adele?" asked Sera. "My goodness, the man has treated you miserably."

"I have my reasons. Anyway, the game is over now. There will be no organist at the Estey again. He's dead," she said bitterly, and Ms. M was surprised to hear what was almost a sob.

"Ms. M, I'm confused. I saw two guys that night. I swear I did." He and Ms. M were sharing cocoa at her house.

"I know. I believe you, Alex." She sighed. "Maybe one of them was Gerald Must. Maybe it was Bob or Colin. We've never considered that possibility. I'm going to drive you home now, Alex. Sleep, think. We'll talk tomorrow."

"Yeah. Okay. I am sleepy." Alex stood up, stretched, and yawned. "One thing. I'm sorry about Max Fox—that he's probably dead, Ms. M. I'm really sorry."

"I know, sweetie. Thank you."

Tasha slept very little that night. She'd never known Max Fox. She'd never even known there was a Max Fox. Why was it so upsetting to know that Max Mulholland's second son was probably dead? He wasn't her child. Still, she'd loved Max and she might have loved this second child of his, this child who was said to have been like his father. She'd always regretted that Stuart wasn't even a little like Max.

She'd never felt guilty about feeling that way, but she did now.

Her other concern was Stuart himself. Now that she knew, with near certainty, that the dead man was Max Fox, she had no choice but to tell him. He could prove beyond a doubt that the man was his stepbrother. He'd be angry with her for not telling him everything sooner. It would be uncomfortable, but that seemed like the least of her problems.

The Organist Who Wore Gloves

A murderer was still among them: Colin, Bob, Cornelia, Gerald Must? Although she could think of no discernible motive, she wondered about Sera, and even Adele.

XXXII

Dear Noah. We're writing to let you know the latest. Our neighbor, Serendipity, who was in love with Max when he was a teenager and she was a child, has claimed several times that Max himself has been playing the organ in the museum. She's a very eccentric woman, and since we had run out of ideas on how to continue this investigation, we agreed to join her in a plan to trap the organist the next time the music sounded. Last night, the three of us went to the museum when the music began. We discovered that the phantom organist was a woman called Adele who is married to Bob Early, Cornelia Early's employer. She was doing it for Bob, who hoped to distract us by making us continue to believe there had been two strangers haunting the museum and that one may have killed the other.

The Organist Who Wore Gloves

This means that Max Fox is almost certainly dead since he was probably always the one and only organist. We're not sure what else it means.

I will be telling my son, Sheriff Mulholland, about our findings. I imagine his investigation will be a lot more of a problem to everyone involved now, especially the murderer.

We're terribly sorry to have to tell you about Max Fox. We know you liked him. Thank you for your interest in our problems. Shrubsbury and the museum must seem terribly remote and strange to you.

Yours, Tasha Mulholland and Alex Churchill

Alex was on his way to the museum, not paying much attention to the road, thinking about being a boy in a small town and how people like Max and Ms. M had lived all over the world. He was restless. His birthday was next week. Thirteen wasn't old enough for anything much, it seemed to him. He couldn't drive. School would still be a bore. He couldn't afford the computer games that would surely give his life more meaning. He and Ms. M were after a deadly murderer—that was exciting—but after they figured it out, he'd still spend his days dusting, weeding and cleaning windows. It took so very long to get to where life could really be lived. Months and months. If he could at least skip a grade....

It wasn't just that he was too young to do all the important things in life. He was even too young to really be a friend to his best friend, Ms. M. He knew she was unhappy about the dead Max Fox. He knew Stuart wasn't much help and never would be. Alex thought the sheriff was kind of a dork. Of course, Alex was comparing him to the TV detectives he knew.

Alex was aware that he could no more tell Ms. M everything about himself than she could tell him about her own thoughts and feelings. It didn't seem fair to either one of them. He could share more about his feelings for the lovely Zoe with Coker, although Coker, too, sometimes seemed to live in another universe than Alex. It was all so complicated. He wanted Zoe, but he didn't know what he meant by that. He wasn't ready to make mad, passionate love to her the way he would be if she were written for TV, even if she would allow it. But why would she? He was still a little kid.

The Organist Who Wore Gloves

But when he saw Zoe, even when he just thought about her, he hurt. Things happened to his body that he couldn't control. None of his TV heroes acted as if they felt that way around beautiful women. They were cool. What was wrong with him anyway? It was the same problem only different as he had with dead bodies. There was an acceptable way to act. He'd seen it done many, many times, but he didn't know how to emulate it. And he knew that if he tried at thirteen, he'd look like a real fool. He was still waiting for his voice to change. He couldn't even disguise himself, surely an important thing to be able to do when you're a detective. Unless, of course, he wanted to pretend he was a girl! Jeeze!

The museum was quiet when he got there. It was a Monday, and Mondays were usually still. Not in cities where there was traffic to beat the band all the time, and thousands of odd people of different colors. Just here. Where there were trees, birds and cows watching him from across the road. The sheriff's car was at Ms. M's. He knew she was probably telling him about his brother, Max Fox. Hell, if Fox was Alex's brother he'd be glad, but he doubted the sheriff was.

Sheriff Stuart Mulholland appeared at the door of the Cyril Benning House and strode to his car, his face grim. Alex watched him from across the road. If he weren't a-not-even-thirteen-year-old yet, he thought, he'd be able to go upstairs and say comforting things to his partner. He'd never seen her cry but he thought she probably was. And there was nothing he could do about it. It was so hard being a kid.

XXXIII

Cornelia's summer camp had been shut up. The table and chairs were gone; the shades were drawn; the doors were locked; the boat had been put away. Tasha walked around, looking for something, anything that would tell her where Cornelia had gone and what her state of mind was. She examined the parking space where the black Impala had stood. The car seemed to have moved out recently; the car tracks were fresh.

Tasha went back to her truck and drove to Colins and Cornelia's house. The windows were closed and the curtains pulled. The garage doors were shut tight. Peeking in the window, she saw the black Impala, but not the green Buick. They were probably together in his car, she thought. She walked around the house, the swimming pool, the garden with its beds of young tulips and daffodils, admiring the stonework that must have cost more than Colin and Cornelia could ever afford. She walked back to her truck and drove to Bob's house.

Tasha hadn't visited the Early home for years, before Bob married Adele, when he lived there with his mother and father, and then just his father. It was a noble old house, Gothic style, a three-story home with a grand staircase. She remembered marveling at the scrollwork on the walls, the chair rail and moldings, the high bookshelves, the massive stone fireplace. The place smelled of honeysuckle in the summer and balsam in the winter.

Tasha rang the bell, waited, and rang again. She took a stone path to the back and discovered Adele lounging poolside. "Adele? You left in such a hurry yesterday evening. I have more questions for you."

"Oh, Lord, it's you again! Why can't you leave me alone?"

"You'll just have to put up with it."

"What the hell do you want to know? Ask me. Then go. Go!" She screwed up her face. She'd moved to the edge of the lounge chair, as if she might get up and run if Ms. M weren't quick to say whatever it was she had to say.

"Why do you think someone killed Max Fox?"

Clearly, that wasn't the question Adele expected. Worse, it wasn't a question she wanted to answer. "Try again. I don't want to speculate about that." Her hands tightened into fists.

"I'd like to know why you're so upset. I just went looking for Cornelia, Colin and Bob. I couldn't find anyone. Not at the camp, not at Colin's house. What's going on?"

"I wouldn't know. They have their own lives. I don't want to know what they're doing. I'm going to make you the first to know, Tasha. I'm divorcing Bob. In fact, I'm divorcing all three of them."

"I can understand that. I can relate to it. Max threw me over for someone years ago. I know exactly how you feel."

"Do you? Yes, I guess you might. What goes around comes around. Isn't that the saying? I'm the bimbo he threw you over for. I'm Belinda."

Tasha staggered visibly, and fell back into a chair. For a moment she just tried to breathe.

"Yeah. I know. You thought I was dead. You were probably glad to hear it. I would have been in your place."

"Why the masquerade? Why are you here?" Tasha finally asked.

"I met Bob a few years ago down south. He was in Richmond for business; he looked me up. I fell in love with him; I married him. Silly me."

"Why did you take another name?"

"I already had. I always hated my given name. Max liked it. He was dead. So I changed it."

"I need a drink."

"We might as well drink." Adele got up, slipped on a robe, and started towards the house. "I'll be right back."

"I'm coming too," said Tasha, afraid the woman would take off and leave her with nothing but confusion and grief.

"Yeah, yeah. I'm not going to run away. But come

on then." Tasha followed the barefoot Adele into the kitchen. "What'll it be?"

"Johnny Walker, rocks. Thank you." Despite her confusion, Tasha found herself really looking at Adele for the first time. Small, slender, younger than she was, of course. Dark hair, dark eyes, perpetual scowl. Another devotee of Johnny Walker.

The two women walked back out to the pool and sat at the faux marble-topped table. The sun colored their faces through a red umbrella.

"I need to know," Tasha said. "Max Fox was your son?"

"Yes. And yes I'm out to do something awful to whoever killed him. I don't know who did it. I've even suspected you. He was a wonderful man."

"We'll do it together," said Tasha. "We'll find who it was together."

Adele looked at her silently, sipping her drink. "You never met him, did you?"

"No. I only caught a glimpse of him. But I loved his father once. I care who did it."

"And your son, his brother, is the sheriff. Stranger than fiction, isn't it? I feel as if I'm in a damn murder mystery."

Tasha smiled ruefully. "Yes. Who do you think killed him?"

"I don't think Bobby did it. I hate him. He and his lovely Cornelia. He'd do anything he could to keep her out of prison if she did it. But he loved Max Sr. and he liked Max Jr. He's not a violent person, even if he's a weasel."

"I'm not as sure of that. He fixed my brakes. You must have suspected him at times."

"Yeah."

"Why?"

"Maxie had something on dear Cornelia. I don't know what. But she felt threatened by him."

"So whatever it was, it was the reason you and Bob thought Cornelia or Colin might have murdered your son."

"Yeah. Except that Colin is such a wuss."

"Is he?"

"Yes. He loans his wife out to his brother. Bob jerks him around, and he just lets him. Total wimp."

"How serious is Bob's affair with Cornelia?"

"Apparently it's been going on for years. He stopped it long enough to marry me. I didn't know, I really didn't. I knew he was attracted to her. But I didn't know they were in that deep. I don't think Colin realized it either. The difference between us is I'm ready to kill Bob, and Colin is prepared to go on living with the situation."

"I'm so sorry, Adele. I had no idea, at least not until Sera told me."

"Yeah, she's another one."

"Another what?"

"Someone I don't trust."

"She'd have no motive to kill your son, would she?"

"Sera doesn't need a motive. She's crazy. She thought he was his father, Max, rejecting her all over again. She might have shot him. She's capable of it."

"So you've been pretending to be her friend just in case."

"Yeah."

"It must have been hard here, getting to know people, making friends."

"It wouldn't have been if I could have trusted my damn husband. You might as well know," Adele said. "I've been in trouble. Nobody but Bob knows who I am. I didn't want to identify Max because I didn't want to call attention to myself."

"That explains why I had so much trouble tracing you and your son. Did Max get his job at Early's Auto because of you?"

"Yeah. I was here. He wanted to look for the secret his father had left. He was hoping for money, but I think he got a kick out of whatever it was, even if it was silly."

"I only know of one more suspect," Tasha said. "What about Gerald Must?"

"I don't know. I don't like him. He hung out with Maxie some. He's been around since, but I don't know why. He pretends to be so damned sick and fragile and then he drives up here and talks to nearly everyone but me. He doesn't like me."

"He doesn't like me either," Tasha said.

The Organist Who Wore Gloves

There was the sound of a smooth expensive engine in the driveway. "Bob's here," said Adele.

"Does he know you're filing for divorce?"

"Oh, yeah. He has a lot to look forward to. I promised him the whole world would know about anything and everything I could find to tell them. I promised I'd hurt his business no matter what, and I'd take every cent I could besides. He'll be happy to see me. Look at him. He's bounding across the grass, eager to greet his darling wife, and who else—his nosy friend who almost certainly knows awful things about his beloved Cornelia. What joy!"

Bob walked over to the two of them and stood looking down at them. He looked tired, Tasha thought. She felt sorry for him, and glad that she'd only experienced one important love in her life, and that it had never turned as sour as his for Cornelia, or as full of betrayal as his relationship with her or Adele.

"Do either of you know where Cornelia and Colin are?"

"I have no idea," said Tasha. "I came here looking for them."

"I see Adele was eager to entertain you."

"She and I have some things in common."

"She's a bitch. Have you noticed, Tasha? You're given to only seeing the good in people, but you must have figured that out."

"Adele hasn't surprised me. I'm afraid I can't say the same for you."

Bob sighed, pulled up a chair and, grabbing Adele's emptied coffee cup, poured himself a jigger of Johnny Walker. "I can't find them," he said. "I don't think they'd run away together. I don't know where they are."

"No, they wouldn't run away from you. Not likely."

"She wrote me a note. She said that she and Colin had to go away to figure something out. She said she was a criminal and she'd been committing a crime against me for years. Tasha, what do you think? Where could they be?"

"I don't know. I looked at the camp and the house. Cornelia wasn't at the museum earlier this morning. I gather she wasn't at work."

"No. Not there. Any guesses?"

The Organist Who Wore Gloves

"Maybe they're trying to work out a financial solution at one bank or another."

"What do you mean?"

"You really don't know, Bob?

"I don't know what you're talking about. A financial solution to what?"

"You're so in love you've never noticed that Cornelia has been robbing you for the last thirty years?"

"Damn! I knew it! I knew it had to be something like that," barked Adele.

"I don't understand," Bob said. "I thought Max Fox might be stealing from the business."

"Cornelia's been embezzling from you for nearly the whole time she's worked at Early's Auto. She guesses that she's taken something like $300,000 from the business. Colin's trying to help her find a way to pay you back."

Bob had turned to stone. "I don't understand," he murmured again.

"Bob, you boob," said Adele, triumphant. "She's been robbing you all these years. A little at a time. You didn't want to see it. You trusted her absolutely you told me. My God, you idiot. You think she loves you, she doesn't even respect you. She's just been afraid you'd find out and turn her in."

"Shut up, you witch," he muttered.

Tasha watched him crumple and grow smaller, his eyes closed, his posture almost fetal. It was sad, she thought. So sad. Still, someone had to tell him, and it was just as well she'd done it and not Colin. Just as well it wasn't Cornelia herself. At least she hoped so.

XXXIV

Alex was sitting quietly in the music room at the museum thinking about the riddle. If he could help Ms. M solve it, maybe they'd figure out who the murderer was. Maybe they'd solve the crime and Ms. M could stop thinking about her past and all the sad people connected with it.

Noah Patrovsky's organ mix of the two unlike pieces of music was not just cool, it was magic, and if Patrovsky could give them that kind of perfectly awesome clue, Alex should be able to solve the riddle.

So he thought about it. The two pieces of music became one. They belonged together. Whatever the clue was it was about the pairing of the two utterly different pieces of music to form one piece (at least for a few bars) or joining their titles to form one thing.

Sugar. Not a sugar bowl. That had been embarrassing, searching the Blue Willow bowl. Searching through all the bowls.

Toccata. A piece of music that danced. The word touch. There was something about that word. There was something about both words. He'd seen the answer somewhere. He just didn't know where.

He stood up and moved around the music room. The answer had to be in this room. It had to be connected to the organ. He walked over and stared at the instrument. The phony pipes, the fancy woodwork, the keys, the pedals…. The bench.

"Alex," called Ms. M from the kitchen door. "Are you there?"

"Yes, I am."

"Wait 'til you hear about my morning." She came into the room.

"Wait 'til you hear what I just figured out," he replied, and walked over to the organ bench. "I think I've got it. I think I know the answer to the riddle."

"In the bench?" she said, surprised.

"Yeah. In an old familiar place," he said and pulled out *Organ Solos for the Beginning Student, The Sweet Touch.*

Ms. M stared down at it. "*The Sweet Touch,*" she murmured. "You may just have got it, Alex Churchill." She smiled at her partner, the kid who was beginning to glow, the kid who had just solved Max Mulholland's puzzle. "Let's go out on the porch where there's more light."

They sat on the porch together, slowly paging through the book, until they found what looked like a page from an old journal, a yellowing paragraph torn from who knows where glued into a page of description, an addendum to a paragraph about the glories of the organ.

"It's Rev. Evensong's handwriting," she said. "We have a few handwritten sermons by him. I've seen it."

"It looks like it might have been a journal page or something. There's a date at the top."

"On this day, October 20, 1834, we finished building the Shrubsbury School, roofing the last of the fourth floor and setting one remaining chimney in place. Cyril and

I came down stairs to celebrate with his good ox, Daisy, who lowed long and loud when we told her her job was done and she'd soon be enjoying the winter in our sweet, warm barn. Mercy and I will hold a community worship and feast on Sunday next to celebrate."

"So there's nothing to the legend that the ox wouldn't or couldn't, come down from the top of the building and was roasted for a community feast and celebration. And that's what this is all about! Oh, Max!"

Ms. Mulholland was laughing, and couldn't stop. "Max, Max. Even after death your sense of humor is marvelous," she said when she could breathe again.

"But that's not important. No one believes that legend, do they?"

"Some people do. Children might. I guess young Max did, and he couldn't bear the disappointment when he discovered this note. It's like keeping the myth of Santa Claus alive by hiding a scientific paper on the physical impossibility of flying reindeer."

Alex was still incredulous. "That's all this is about. The phantom playing the organ. The guy haunting the museum."

"At least one part of the mystery has been solved. It doesn't explain anything about the murder, but it may help us speculate in some way we can't quite see yet. I'm going to put it back for safekeeping, Alex."

"But what if someone else finds it?"

"I think Max Fox had already. This way no one will know we have."

Ms. M drove Alex home and told him about her meeting with Adele and Bob, soft pedaling the sexual aspects of everything as much as she was able, forgetting that he'd seen much worse on television many times. He listened, but he didn't really care because the riddle was so lame. They'd solved it and it was silly. He wasn't proud anymore. He just felt stupid.

Why had Ms. M found it so funny? Would it be as funny to Noah Patrovsky as it was to Ms. M? Maybe he didn't have as much in common with old people as he'd thought.

That night, Alex wrote to Mr. Patrovsky, just as Ms. M had told him to.

Dear Mr. Patrovsky, We've found the answer to Max's riddle. Thank you so much for your part in helping us solve it. The reference the tunes-made-into-one-tune pointed to was in the organ bench all along. It referred to an old book of instruction for the reed organ entitled The Sweet Touch. *The solution involved nothing monetary or even especially valuable, just the dissolution of an old legend that belongs to the Old Shrubsbury School Museum.*

Thank you so much for your help. We're guessing that you didn't know what the answer was any more than we did. Alex thinks the whole thing is disappointing in the extreme.

We've talked to you about the Early brothers and Cornelia Early before. We think one of them murdered Max Fox. Almost as likely, Gerald Must could have done it. We'd like to know what your opinion is.

Yours, Alex and Ms. Mulholland

XXXV

Tasha got started early the next day. She wanted to find Cornelia and Colin before Bob did. She was afraid that one of the Early brothers would confess the crime when it was really Cornelia who had done it. She was surprised when she discovered Alex sitting in the truck waiting for her.

"I thought you were off this silly case," she said.

"Almost. But I can't believe there's nothing more to it than we already know."

"So you're coming with me?"

"Yep."

"You realize it must be this way sometimes in the life of every detective? The mystery turns out to have had a cut and dried solution all along."

"Yeah. Maybe."

"Do you have any ideas about where Cornelia and Colin went?"

"No ma'am. Do you think they've been visiting banks looking for loans?"

"That was the implication of the note they left Bob, but that's not how you look for loans as a rule."

"Ms. M, even if we found them how would we get them to tell the truth? We don't know when Max Fox died so we can't check alibis."

"You're right, Alex. It's kind of dispiriting, isn't it? Unless one of them gets angry enough at the others to identify the killer, we're kind of stuck."

"Are you going to tell your son about Mrs. Early embezzling?"

"I don't know. He's awfully mad at me right now. Besides, I don't know if that information would help him solve the murder. Unless Bob decides to file charges, I don't even know if it matters. It's a crime that's kind of all in the family."

"Everybody in town would be pretty disgusted with her if they knew."

"Yes. It would be harder for her to live here, wouldn't it? Bob has been terribly hurt by it. He may not forgive her. I wonder if he's found them yet."

They found Bob pacing the deck at the camp. Ms. M and Alex walked up the boardwalk together. Bob saw them coming and sat down, facing them.

"Hello," he said. "Isn't it time you gave up? I doubt any of us killed Max Fox."

"I thought you were concerned that Colin or Cornelia might have."

"I'm way past that now. All I can think of is what she did. And that he knew."

"Not the whole time."

"How could it take him that long? The bastard."

"You're not so fast at figuring things out yourself, Bob."

"Yeah. Touché." He stared across the pond at nothing. Water birds called. A breeze ruffled the surface of the water. New dragonflies spun over the sparkling surface. Bob didn't see any of it. "I heard from her last night. She said she missed me."

Tasha shook her head sadly.

"Is there any reason why they'd be down in southern Vermont?"

"Is that where they are?"

"Yeah. Somewhere down there. She used a land phone, not her cell. She's lost her cell. Here, Tasha. Tell me if that phone number is familiar?" He held out his phone for her to see. Alex asserted himself by taking a look too.

"Wow," he said. "Do you see what I see, Ms. M?"

"I think I do, Alex. Did she say they were still looking for money?" she asked Bob.

"Yeah. That's what it sounded like."

"Well, if it's any consolation, if that's who we think it is, he has lots of money. We're late, Alex. Shall we go?"

"Yeah. We should."

They stopped at Alex's mother's nursery on the way to the highway, and Tasha explained that something had just come up, that they were going to pick up an important heirloom for the museum collection from

Noah Patrovsky at Brattleboro. She could really use Alex's help carrying it, and he'd so enjoyed his visit with the old man the last time.... They'd be back late tonight.

Donna Churchill said "Yes, of course. Have a wonderful time."

Sera looked up from where she stood pricing a variety of euphorbia. She'd overheard the conversation and arrived at her own interpretation. Ms. Mulholland and Alex were excited and on their way to Brattleboro. They were about to solve the murder of Max Fox. She pulled her cellphone from her cleavage and called Adele.

Not long after, Ms. M and Alex were on the highway in the red truck heading south.

They were about halfway there, somewhere around Lake Morey, when Alex said, "Remember when we had lunch at Noah Patrovsky's house? And after lunch... "

"Yes, and after his speech about breaking rules...."

"Yeah. I just remembered. He went out for a smoke."

"Camels?"

"I don't know."

"Of course, he's 101 years old and unlikely to drive all the way to Shrubsbury to shoot someone, push the body into the water, dispose of a car, and return a bike to the house where it belonged."

"Yeah. Pretty far-fetched, huh?"

"Still, he does smoke," she said.

Ms. M borrowed Alex's phone to call her son, the sheriff.

XXXVI

Noah Patrovsky's house was lit up. Light poured out of the windows as if there were so much of it inside it couldn't be contained. Patrovsky's marvelous assistant, Jeanette, opened the door to Alex and Ms. Mulholland. "Come in, come in," she said, as if they were expected.

They followed her down the hallway, through the arboretum and into the library and music room. Colin and Cornelia were sitting together on the sofa Alex and Ms. M had sat on so many days ago. Across from them, in a great red chair that could have passed for a throne, sat Noah Patrovsky in a black silk kimono, smiling broadly. "Good afternoon Ms. Mulholland. Mr. Churchill."

"Hi, Mr. Patrovsky," said Alex. "We didn't know you knew Mr. and Mrs. Early."

"Ah, but of course, I do."

"Good afternoon, Noah," said Ms. Mulholland. "Alex and I are pleased that you're going to help Cornelia pay back Early's Auto. We decided to come and share in the general hilarity."

"And that is what it is. You understand me, Tasha. We're celebrating. Cornelia made a mistake, and since I'm grotesquely rich, I'm happy to help her remedy it."

"He's been very kind, Tasha."

"A low interest loan?"

"Yes."

"Covering the whole debt?"

"Yes."

Someone came into the room behind them. Noah Patrovsky smiled broadly. "Bob, hello. Look who's just arrived—he must have followed you, Tasha. Bob. Did you hear? We're going to make sure you get every cent back."

"Yeah," murmured Bob. "So kind." He was staring at Cornelia, his eyes burning, his fists tightening, his shoulders tensing. Cornelia looked back at him. She seemed stunned, wounded, as if his gaze were a machine gun and he was aiming, firing, shooting.

"Now," Patrovsky continued, "Bob, Tasha, Mr. Churchill—before we move this party along any further, let me do my duty as your host. You'll notice there's a bar on the far wall beneath the likeness of Dionysius. I think you'll find everything there you need or could ever want. Bob, you might as well do this sad scene with good whiskey. I think you'll be impressed by what I'm offering. Cornelia and Colin, feel free to replenish your drinks. I expect you'll need fortification. For those of you who are—by reason of youth or some other infirmity—abstinent, there are soft drinks on ice."

It was like a *Double 007* movie, Alex thought. As he took a bottle from the ice bucket, he knew he'd never have a Coke like this one again. It wasn't alcoholic, but he was sure it would seem as if it were. Standing in front of the dark wood and mirrors, he admired the bottles of amaretto, cointreau, crème de cassis, grenadine, kahlua—every one of them a different shape and size and shining like a jewel, and their reflections twinkling in the faceted glass. The larger bottles of bourbon, gin, Scotch whiskey, tequila, and vodka were arranged like books next to them. How would he ever be able to drink them all when he grew old enough?

Cornelia had sidled up to Bob as he poured himself a double shot of a Macallan single malt he knew he'd never see again in this life. The old man was right. He might as well get through this in style. He looked at her somberly, but he didn't really see her. She wasn't the woman he'd loved for a lifetime.

"Bob, I'm sorry. I didn't know how to tell you. I've never known how to tell you."

He shrugged and looked for a seat, choosing a black leather recliner designed for one person. It was fortified. There was no way a second person could share it. It was hard for a second person to even approach it.

Cornelia went back to the bar where Colin stood waiting for her with a full wine glass in either hand. She stayed close to him as they made their way back to the soft, soft sofa Alex and Ms. M remembered so well.

Feeling small and displaced, Alex lingered at the bar near Ms. M who had poured herself something more expensive than Johnny Walker Red. She smiled at him. "Shall we go find the two best seats in the house?" she said. They headed for a chaise lounge the same red as

The Organist Who Wore Gloves

Noah's massive chair and, as Jeanette appeared with a tray of canapés, settled in for what they were certain would be a show like none they'd ever seen before.

"What shall we do first?" Noah asked. "Bob, Cornelia?" He hesitated. "Colin. You've said very little. I imagine that's always the case with you, but here—here's a chance to say what you're feeling. You may never have another opportunity like this one."

"You're right, Noah. I should say something to Bob." He stood up and turned to look at his brother. "You must forgive her, Bob. She never meant to cheat you. It became a habit she didn't know how to break. And I, I didn't know. I really didn't until a few weeks ago. We both love you. You know that. And now you're to have your money back."

"I don't care about the money," growled Bob.

"Please, Bob," said Cornelia in a near whisper. "Please forgive me. I'll do whatever you want. Please."

"Thirty years, and you never choked on the words, 'I love you.' You just kept taking."

"I was afraid to tell you. For thirty years, I've been afraid."

"Afraid of me. Now, you have reason to be afraid. Then, you never did."

"I thought you'd always love her," Colin said. "I didn't know you could stop."

"Neither did I. I didn't know I could hate my brother either. I've found out all sorts of things about myself in the last twenty-four hours. Do you know how I've tried to protect you both—the minute I thought there was a chance that either of you had killed that guy? Adele's son. That stupid, stupid kid. I would have died for either one of you."

Colin sank into himself; he didn't say anything else.

"What drama," declared Noah, rubbing his hands together in delight. "What wonderful drama."

Jeeze, thought Alex. He's wicked. I didn't know. The old man is absolutely wicked. He was confused. He'd seen emotional scenes on television and in the movies, but this was real, he guessed. Then again, for a moment he thought they might all be acting. He sneaked a look at Ms. M's face. She had tears in her eyes. My God! Maybe it was real.

"More guests have arrived," said Noah. "When I

realized we were going to have this peculiar celebration, I thought everyone might come. All but Max Fox, of course. I'm glad to see them—every one." He gestured toward the doorway where Adele and Sera stood. "Please, ladies. Help yourselves to drinks and come join us."

The afternoon sun was low in the sky; the light lay in the room in slabs of color. Even though emotions were raw and high, except for the ticking of a clock, the room was silent. No one knew what to say; no one knew what was coming next. "The light is beautiful, isn't it?" said Noah. "I've always loved this time of day."

Adele moved quickly to the bar and began mixing herself a vodka and tonic. In her low sharp-edged voice, she declared, "I only came, Noah Patrovsky, because I was told that my son's murderer would be revealed. You know what I think of all of you. Please get on with it."

Sera had sunk down into a seat on the other side of the room. The light turned her purple dress to a rich churchly purple. Her dark red hair gleamed like fire. She was from space, thought Alex. Another galaxy.

This was turning into a scene from a comic book.

"Ah, yes," said Noah. "Your son, Max Fox. Dear Belinda, if he'd been a little less of a nuisance to all of us, he might have lived to a ripe old age. But I'm not sure you're going to find the answer you're looking for here, tonight. What do you think, Ms. Mulholland? You and Alex Churchill are supposed to be detectives. Do you think we'll learn who Max's murderer is today?"

"Yes, I do. Not immediately, but soon."

"My, my. I'm surprised, and looking forward to your solution."

At just that moment and with a flourish, Stuart arrived, swinging the door open, standing in the doorway, his legs spread, one hand on his holstered gun. Alex had never realized he had so much showman in him. "It's the gendarmes. What superb timing," exclaimed Noah. "May I offer you a drink, Sheriff?"

Stuart stayed as he was, stalwart, sober. "No, thank you, Mr. Patrovsky. I don't drink on the job. And I am on the job."

"Ho! You think, like your mother, that you're going to uncover the culprit. How wonderful."

"So all of you, get down to it," said Adele. "My son

went to Shrubsbury to solve the riddle his father left him. He hoped the solution would be worth some money. There was no reason for him to die."

"The riddle proved to be worth nothing, so he got ambitious and tried to blackmail Cornelia," said Colin.

"Blackmail? That's why he'd turned threatening, and that's why one of you killed him?" exclaimed Bob.

"Oh, come on, Bob. Neither of us killed the guy. You know me. I'd never kill anyone."

"Yeah. Not as a rule. You haven't spine enough for murder. But for her you'd do anything."

"Neither of us would kill anyone. Please, Bob...." Cornelia said.

"Oh, I don't know. I think you're both capable," Bob said with a mean grin.

Alex watched Noah. Did he think any of the Earlys were capable of murder? The old man was watching the altercation the way a fan watches a game: looking at Bob, then Cornelia and Colin, then Bob again, his small dark eyes sparkling. "So, Ms. Mulholland, which one of them do you think did it?"

"We have no evidence that an Early killed Max Fox."

"So maybe the killer is a Mr. Must."

From somewhere near the great pipe organ, Gerald Must stood up. He'd been there the whole time, unnoticed. Dressed in brown pinstripes, he looked like the furniture—perhaps a rail back chair. A slender armoir. He limped across the room, his cane swinging, moving directly to the bar where he mixed himself a martini, apparently not his first, and stood in a lopsided posture, watching everybody, his face painted with the same sour expression Alex remembered.

"Gerald Must. Did you do it?"

"No. I blackmailed Mrs. Early. But I didn't murder anyone," he said and sipped his drink.

"So you found out from Max that Cornelia was an embezzler?" asked Tasha.

"Yes. Not long after Max settled in Shrubsbury and began his quixotic search for the answer to his father's riddle."

"And you left Cornelia threatening letters and finally collected a considerable sum from her?"

"Yes. That was after Max's demise. I figured I had her on two counts then—embezzlement and murder. I planned on asking for more."

"Did you just assume she'd murdered Max, or did you have proof?"

"I assumed it—but surely you can all see that it's obvious?"

"I think it's more likely you did it," said Tasha.

"Why would I?"

"Because you wanted to blackmail her and take everything; you didn't want to share any of the takings with Max Fox."

"You're right that he and I were partners in blackmail."

"Maxie wouldn't have worked with you, you bastard!" Adele exclaimed from across the room. "He hated you and you hated him."

"It didn't matter. I've never liked anybody very much, Belinda. Of course, I hated him, but we had a business deal. He wasn't like his father—full of silly, sweet ideals. We made a bargain and we would have gone through with it together if he hadn't been killed by some idiot."

"You may have never liked anyone very much, Gerald Must," said Tasha. "But I think Adele is right. Max didn't like you. He wouldn't have made a bargain with you. I may be prejudiced because I knew his father, but I don't think Max tried to blackmail Cornelia. I think she thought he had. He knew about her embezzlement. But you're the one who blackmailed her. I asked my son, Sheriff Mulholland, to check and see if you'd made a large deposit in the amount of 10,000 dollars to your bank account in the last few weeks. You had."

Gerald Must scowled. "Believe what you will about the blackmail. But you have no proof that I murdered the boy."

"You're right. And I don't think you did." Like the case, the room was turning dark. The sun was setting; everyone was dimmed. They all looked guilty in the lengthening shadows.

Noah Patrovsky turned on the chandelier above him with a remote in the arm of his chair, and stood up, laughing. "That's why I don't think you're going to find your murderer, Tasha Mulholland. All your suspects say they couldn't possibly have done it, and you have no hard evidence to convict any of them."

Ms. M smiled. "I'm not sure we have evidence that will stand up in a court of law, but that won't be necessary if I'm right about who did the killing. Alex and I think we know who the murderer is. I may even have some notion of why he did it."

"Do go on, Ms. Mulholland," Noah Patrovsky said, and sat down again. At the bar, Adele helped herself to a second vodka and tonic and fixed one more for Serendipity who had, uncharacteristically, not said a word.

"A few days ago, Alex found the answer to the riddle Max Mulholland posed decades ago when he was still a youngster. His son, Max, had solved it a few weeks before. He realized that it was an amusing, but not especially valuable gift. I don't know if he was annoyed by the fact. It was difficult, I think, for him to just leave afterwards. His mother was nearby, even though the two of them were estranged. The museum was full of his father. Both Gerald Must and Mr. Patrovsky knew he was in Shrubsbury. Must had visited him and learned about Cornelia's embezzlement. He didn't tell Must about the substance of the riddle because Gerald Must didn't care. The minute he heard that nothing monetary would come of it, he let Max Fox know he didn't care.

"Mr. Patrovsky, on the other hand, did care. He enjoyed a good riddle and especially a musical one. He was pleased with Max's solution and they played the two pieces of music that figure in it together on at least one occasion. Later, Noah found pleasure in passing the clue on to us. We were grateful, and I know Alex couldn't have found the solution without it."

Alex nodded and smiled his most charming smile at the old man in the great red chair.

"Perhaps our little group here would enjoy hearing what we're talking about," Noah said.

Someone who didn't love music groaned.

Noah Patrovsky pulled himself up out of his chair and ambled in his spidery way to the huge pipe organ on the other side of the room, climbed up onto the bench and began his performance of the "Toccata and Fugue." Everyone stiffened to attention, their chins raised, inspired without any intention of being so, until Noah added the first notes of "Sugar," looking out at his audience with the broadest and happiest of smiles. Some of them returned his grin and began tapping their feet. Others looked annoyed. The interruption of the "Toccata" was too abrupt. It hurt in some indefinable way. It broke the rules.

Patrovsky stopped. Alex just managed to stop himself from applauding. The old organist carefully climbed down from the instrument that was his mountain, and sat on a simple straight-backed chair next to it. He pulled a pack of cigarettes and a lighter from the sleeve of his kimono, and lit up. Alex couldn't help himself; he laughed out loud.

Tasha smiled gently. "Noah, you're the only one Max shared his riddle with. No one else cared (except, perhaps, for myself and Alex and we didn't know him then). You shot him—and I admit this is pure speculation—after the two of you played the music together on the reed organ at the museum. You and Max Fox went out onto the dock so you could have a cigarette, a Camel as it turned out. You had disposed of butts in at least two other places—where Max left his bicycle and by the door of the building where you waited while he wrote his poetry. Alex collected them. Sheriff Mulholland had them tested.

"Tasha, I can't believe you're accusing me of murder. A 101-year-old man. How would I have pushed the body into the water? How would I have taken the bicycle back to where it belonged? You can't imagine I would have ridden it. How did I dispose of Max Fox's car?

"And why would I have done it?"

"I'm not sure of the answers to the first three questions, but as you have a lot of money Noah, I'm sure it wasn't hard to do. I have an answer to the last question. You gave it to Alex and me when we visited you here. It's very simple. It's become a hobby of yours to break as many rules as you can before you die."

Noah Patrovsky looked at her and smiled sweetly. "Well done, Ms. Mulholland. But you don't have the evidence to convict me any more than you do anyone else. And as you said earlier, before I came to trial I'd almost certainly die. So, Sheriff Mulholland, you might as well put those handcuffs away. You're not going to arrest a man as old as I am on the basis of so little proof. It is, as I said, Tasha. When all is said and done, you have no evidence that anyone in this room murdered Max Fox."

"What kind of human being are you?" Adele said, rising, her voice low and threatening. "You wanted to break all the rules and so you shot my boy? He wasn't a friend, he was a rule to break?" She was holding her arms straight out, a pistol in one hand. "Are you ready to die now? Tonight?"

The Sheriff started toward her, his hand on the handle of his revolver. "No, Sheriff," said Sera. She stood between Adele and Sheriff Mulholland, filling the space with color. "Let her do it. It's only just."

"Stuart," said Tasha. "Be careful."

"Well, well," said Noah Patrovsky. "Oddly enough, I don't want to die at the hands of this woman. This terrible woman. She's cheap and mean. She's sour. I have my own ideas of what my death should be like."

"Tough," said Serendipity. "Shoot him. Quick!"

Adele did. But she didn't allow for the nimbleness of the old man she wanted to shoot. Noah fell limp as a dead body to the floor and rolled under a couch. The bullet struck the organ behind him. The Sheriff stepped around Sera and took the gun from Adele. Two-gunned, he commanded Noah to stand up. But a 101-year-old man moves very, very slowly and no one was sure how long it might take.

XXXVII

It was Alex's birthday. It should have been a special day. He shouldn't have had to work. There should have been balloons! His mother should have done more than give him a kiss, a hug and a happy birthday card in the morning, with a promise of a present later in the month when she got paid. Ms. M should have made his favorite ginger cookies and told him how much older he looked. She should have played a special piece of music for him on her cello. Coker should have invited him to play the latest version of Star Wars: The Force Unleashed II on his computer.

Alex wasn't dumb. He knew that there was probably a party for him scheduled for later in the day—a party with lots of balloons, a new bicycle, a cookie jar

The Organist Who Wore Gloves

full of ginger cookies, and "Happy Birthday" played on a cello. He knew Coker would be there and they'd start a new game of Star Wars. No, it wasn't that he didn't think he'd get a birthday party. It was that he wanted something besides that. He wasn't even sure what.

Maybe he wanted some assurance that thirteen was much older than twelve, and, in fact, nearly grown. Maybe he wanted someone to tell him his life would be different this year. He wanted an adult conversation with Ms. M, and an unusual song, something made especially for him. He didn't care much about a new bicycle. He didn't want to play video games tonight. He wanted balloons, but he wanted them set loose in the sunset of the day, like small flames. For the first time in his life, he was particular about his birthday and how he celebrated it.

He was surprised when Ms. M stopped him just as he started to mow the last quarter of the lawn. "Alex, I need you for a little while. Can you let the mowing go until later?"

"Sure. With pleasure."

He followed her to her house. "How would you like to go on a hike before your surprise party? Just you and me."

"Hey, that would be great."

"Maybe up Mt. Pisgah?"

"That would be perfect."

"We could get Coker to come with us if you want, but I thought it might be more fun if it was just you and me."

"Yeah, that's how I'd like it too."

"Great. I'm going to put a lunch together for us, including some of the ginger cookies I made for you last night."

So it was that that afternoon they headed up Pisgah, high above Lake Willoughby, where the rocks were piled up on all sides, like the walls of old churches and wildflowers spotted the cliffs like jewels.

"You're doing pretty good for an old lady, Ms. M," said Alex.

"Not bad, huh. I think you and I can go on some more walks together. I thought we should talk about our partnership, Alex. You've seen some pretty awful things this last year. Are you okay?"

"Yeah. I mean the bodies bother me, but I think

what's worse are the people. I mean I thought that guy Noah was great and he turned out to be a jerk. Nobody is really nice, you know. Just you and me and maybe Coker.

"And your mother."

"Yeah…. Of course."

"The other thing is that we're both changing, especially you. You're becoming a young man. How do you feel about hanging out with an old lady? I know it must not seem very cool."

She didn't expect him to answer her right away while he looked at the world below them getting wider and wider, and the lake smaller. She let him find the words.

"I kid you not, Ms. M. Sometimes, it's uncomfortable. I know girls who hang out with their grandmothers. But you're not even a grandma. And I'm not a girl. It's always been that way a little. It's been harder lately. But you're my best friend. So, that's the way it is."

"I'm glad. It's like that for me too, you know. You're not my grandson, but you are just about my favorite person. I know it's been hard for you lately because

I haven't told you everything. I probably won't until you're nearly grown. I know you don't tell me things either. That's okay. We'll just have to put up with each other until our ages change some more and I'm not much older, but you are."

Alex laughed. "Okay. I'm waiting for nearly everything else. I'll wait for that too."

They sat on a high rock and ate lunch. Clouds flew like bright white birds in front of the sun, and away again. Ravens called to each other about the weather; crows quarreled. Far above them, a hawk circled silently. Alex thought how good it was to be part of everything.

The surprise party was waiting at the museum when they got back. Everyone sang "Happy Birthday," not once but several times. Alex pretended his astonishment and accepted his new bike enthusiastically. Zoe helped send the balloons up, so he had every excuse to study her. What a woman, he thought. Thirteen is so young. Why did he have to be so young? At least, he was headed in the right direction. More years, not less.

He was pleased when Sheriff Mulholland showed up, said "Happy Birthday," and thanked him for

The Organist Who Wore Gloves

helping to solve the case of the organist who wore gloves.

"You're sure that Noah Patrovsky did it then?" asked Alex.

"Pretty sure. I don't think he'll do any time. He didn't get bail; the judge just sent him home. One hundred and one years. What else could he do?"

Alex shrugged his shoulders. "Thanks for letting me know, Sheriff Mulholland," he said. Being a year older was beginning to pay off.

He and Ms. M got an e-mail from Noah Patrovsky that evening.

Happy birthday, Mr. Churchill. I hope you live as many years as I have, and more.

If somebody had to find the killer, I'm glad it was you two.

Yours, Noah Patrovsky.

Made in the USA
Charleston, SC
06 December 2012